"I'm going to be back on top again."

There was pride in Ben's words. "And I'm going to take you with me, Ellie."

Ellie felt dazed and numb as Ben Kolter ran his thumb seductively across her hand. That nasty little song about her was being played from Boston to L.A.

"You're making a fool of me in order to promote your record," she snapped, pulling away from him. "And I'm not going to allow it."

"What can you do about it?" Kolter challenged. "Complain about me to your viewers?"

She met his eyes with a cold anger that went deeper than anything she'd ever felt before. He had gained her confidence then betrayed it.

"No, Mr. Kolter. I'm not going to give you any free airtime. I'm going to slap an injunction on that song."

She was going to hit him where it hurt, and it was what she wanted. Wasn't it?

SHARRON COHEN is happily married. In fact, her husband is the role model for all her heroes, although, she says candidly, he doesn't dress as well as most of them. This American author from Massachusetts, in addition to her romance-novel writing, has written a local newspaper column about children and has done short-story writing for a magazine.

Books by Sharron Cohen

HARLEQUIN ROMANCE
2839—ODD MAN OUT

SHARRON COHEN

high country

Harlequin Books

TORONTO • NEW YORK • LONDON
AMSTERDAM • PARIS • SYDNEY • HAMBURG
STOCKHOLM • ATHENS • TOKYO • MILAN

Harlequin Presents first edition October 1987
ISBN 0-373-11015-4

Original hardcover edition published in 1987
by Mills & Boon Limited

CHAPTER ONE

THE WIND whipped down from the mountain peaks, carrying the kind of icy winter chill that caused a gnawing ache deep within the bones.

Eleanora Martin sat inside her car, rubbing her hands together from anxiety as well as cold. She'd been here for an hour without seeing another car along the deserted stretch of highway, and she knew she might be here for hours to come before anyone passed by.

She could take no comfort from the hope that she'd be missed. Although she lived with her father, they were so accustomed to following different schedules that she could be away for days before he'd notice she was gone. She'd be missed if she didn't show up for work, but since she didn't have to report to the television station until the following evening, that didn't help her now. She was probably going to spend the night here on the deserted road, Ellie realised gloomily, searching through her glove compartment for a warmer pair of mittens. As soon as the sun brushed the mountains with the first feeble glow of a winter sunrise she would get out and walk, but until then she'd have to find a way to keep calm in the claustrophobic confines of the car.

She knew it would be foolish to waste her

battery running the heater until she really needed it, and it would be even more foolhardy to drain the remaining energy for the radio, but she thought that she'd go crazy if all she had to listen to was the eerie keening of the wind. So she reached out and clicked it on.

'. . . at Duchin's Steak House . . .' It fizzed and crackled into life. '. . . where the drinks are cold and the music is hot enough to warm a country cowboy's heart. And speaking of country cowboys, we're doing a Ben Kolter retrospective tonight, starting with his new release: *Eleanora*, by Ben Kolter's Travelling Asylum Band. We're dedicating it, of course, to the frosty beauty who inspired it, Eleanora Martin, the entertainment critic for television station WQBX in Boulder.'

Ellie didn't miss the irony of the dedication as she pulled her fur-edged hood around her face and hunched down on the seat. The announcer had no idea just how frosty that particular beauty was tonight.

A bare second later, four rowdy voices filled her car with the exuberance of their tasteless song. 'I watch the news for Eleanora . . . She won't tell me any lies . . . I watch the news for Eleanora . . . And I undress her with my eyes . . .'

The song was an accounting of Eleanora Martin's charms—the corn-blonde hair that she kept neatly wrapped in a bun at the nape of her long neck, her clear green eyes and wide, full lips, and the shapely body she tried to hide beneath her wardrobe of chic tailored suits. All of it was delivered in a brashly suggestive manner by a group of misfit country singers.

'Take your hair down, Eleanora . . .' It was Ben Kolter's voice that sang the solos, and his clear baritone vibrated with a sensual promise that lifted the song at times from parody to outright proposition. 'I don't mean you any harm . . . Let me kiss you, Eleanora . . . Become a woman in my arms . . .'

That pretty much summed up Ben Kolter's view of the universe, Ellie guessed, irritated that the Colorado cowboy didn't think she'd be a woman until she had experienced the pleasures that he offered. He *was* attractive. She'd admit that much. But her taste in men was a little more refined than anyone she could find in Boulder. It certainly was far more refined than *him*.

'*Eleanora.*' The announcer's voice came on as smooth as satin in the darkness of the night. 'That's the first song Ben Kolter has recorded since his comeback from a ten-year retirement, and it was inspired by a long-standing feud between the Travelling Asylum Band and Eleanora Martin of station WQBX . . .'

Long-standing feud? Ellie's eyebrows lifted at the news. She had given the band an unfavourable review when they had played a benefit at the Boulder Coliseum. A few weeks later, *Eleanora* had appeared on the radio, to everyone's amusement except hers. She couldn't deny a surge of distaste whenever she heard Ben Kolter's smutty little song, but that hardly constituted a long-standing feud.

The local newspaper had been the first to suggest the whole idea of a personal vendetta between her and the band, but Eleanora knew better than to respond to any of their questions. If she attacked the song, it would sell another thousand copies. If she ignored it, it would eventually sink into the obscurity to which it rightfully belonged.

'We're going back fifteen years for our next song. *Truck Stop Love* was the first Ben Kolter song to make it to the charts, and that was . . .' Ellie snapped off the radio, wincing as the bitter wind gusted down from the nearby mountain peaks, rattling her tiny car as if it were no more substantial than a toy. Pulling her fur-edged hood more closely around her face, she craned her neck to peer behind her along the deserted highway.

It was then she saw the headlights, two white moons of light that cut a swathe before them through the inky blackness of the night. She hurried out of the car and waved her arms above her head just as a pickup truck rattled past her on the rutted road. To her great relief, it stopped several yards ahead, then backed up along the shoulder of the road.

The door swung open, letting out a man along with a rush of music from his blaring radio. 'What's wrong?' he demanded, approaching with his hands shoved deep into the pockets of his sheepskin coat to protect them from the bitter blast of cold.

'I don't know,' answered Ellie, wishing she could see the man's face more clearly in the darkness, but he wore a broad-brimmed Stetson hat which hid his features even more completely than the shadows of the night. All she could see was the heavy sheepskin coat that made him seem terrifyingly powerful as he stopped beside her. She was alone on a deserted road, and this could be the worst kind of man with the worst kind of ideas about a stranded woman. He wasn't, she told herself pragmatically, trying to push the sudden fear aside. He had stopped to help her, nothing more. 'I was driving along and I heard a sound—sort of a "chunka-chunka"—and then the car died.'

'Chunka-chunka?' The man was just a touch amused.

'Something like that,' she admitted sheepishly. 'All I know about cars is how to turn the key in the ignition.'

'Then you should stay away from roads like this when you're driving alone,' he cautioned grimly, returning to the front of her car and lifting up the hood. 'Nice car,' the man changed the subject as he crouched over her engine and squinted in the darkness. 'It's a Lamborghini, isn't it?'

'Yes.'

'You don't see many Lamborghinis here in Colorado,' the man kept up a conversation as he poked and prodded, examining the metallic entrails like a surgeon. 'It's hard to drive them over from Italy. They keep filling up with water. That was a joke,' he explained when Ellie didn't answer. 'I thought you might appreciate a little humour right now.' He didn't seem to demand a response, and Ellie didn't give one. 'How long have you been out here?' he changed the subject again as he bent down to touch a wire.

'About an hour and a half.'

'Hm.' He gave the wire a shake, then pushed it down to firm it into its connection. 'No wonder you're not laughing at my jokes. You must be close to freezing!'

Ellie stood helplessly aside, embarrassed by the fears that had flickered briefly into life. There was something comforting about the way he had so quickly turned his attention to her car. And there had been something else that had put her at ease as well. The man's voice, Ellie realised, trying to decipher why it seemed so reassuringly familiar. Low and sensual and laced with a wry, good-natured humour, it was utterly attractive.

'I don't suppose you have a tool-kit in this fancy buggy?' the man asked without looking up from the engine.

'Yes.' Ellie was relieved to be given something she could do. She searched through her trunk until she found the tool-kit and a flashlight, then she returned to the front of the car.

Music poured from the open door of the pickup truck, and the man was singing along with it as he nudged the wires with an exploring hand. 'Forever isn't what it used to be . . . Forever used to be a little longer . . .'

'Shine that flashlight over here,' he instructed as he opened the tool-kit and selected a socket wrench. 'Forever used to mean a thing or two . . .' He continued his distracted singing. 'Back when your love for me was stronger . . .'

Ellie shone the flashlight on the engine, staring incredulously at the face that was illuminated at the outer edge of the flashlight's glowing circle. It was Ben Kolter's face, lean and taut, but romantically attractive. No wonder she had recognised his voice! She had every reason to recognise his low seductive baritone and his sarcastic wit since she had had the dubious honour of being on the receiving end of both.

Of all the men in Colorado who could have stopped to help her, it was this one who leaned across her engine. Ellie pulled her hood more tightly around her recognisable face, wondering what his reaction would be if he knew who she was. She was the woman who had told thousands of people that his songs had no more musical sophistication than rain beating on a metal roof.

On the other hand, he had certainly given her a dose of public humiliation with his rowdy, tasteless song. That made them more than equal. And, despite what he might feel about her, Ellie knew instinctively that he wouldn't leave her here. There was a code of honour even in the modern West. No man would leave a woman stranded on a highway on a bitter night like this.

'You sing very nicely,' Ellie complimented, glancing across his broad shoulder at the mysteries of the engine. 'Better than whoever that is on the radio.'

'Kolter,' he answered with a distracted grunt.

'Oh, yes.' She pretended to recognise the name now that he had said it. 'He's the one who wrote that song about the reporter, Eleanora Martin.' The man didn't answer, and Ellie decided to press further. 'I love her reviews. I think *she's* wonderful.'

'Hm.' He gave the socket wrench a yank to tighten the bolt beneath it. 'If you like the iceberg type.'

Iceberg type? Ellie glared at the man's back. Was that what he thought of her? She had developed a distinctive style, one that depended on a reserved dignity and a certain aloofness, but she was hardly the frosty, hard-edged woman that some people thought she was.

'I don't think she's cold,' she disagreed.

'Are you kidding?' Kolter answered. 'A man could get frostbite touching someone like her. *If* a man could get close enough to touch her. Those cold green eyes of hers would stop a man before he got within ten yards. Her daddy owns half of Colorado, and it's a good thing, too. I've heard that without her daddy's money Eleanora Martin would be just another uppity, bleached blonde.'

'Is that what you've heard?' Ellie answered coolly, forcing the flashlight to remain steady in her trembling hand. She'd lived with rumours all her life, but she'd never learned to shrug them off the way some people could. No matter how talented and hard-working she was, someone was always going to claim that every success had been bought with her father's money. If she dressed well people would claim that she was flaunting what she had, but if she dressed plainly they would claim that she was pretending to be someone that she wasn't. Shyness was called snobbery. Dedication to her job was ruthless, raw ambition. There was no way to win.

But the worst part of it all was that people believed the rumours. This man obviously did. 'I've heard that Ben Kolter thinks Tchaikovsky is a brand of Russian vodka,' she suggested pointedly.

'Rich, spoiled, and cold as a mountain lake in the dead of January,' Kolter continued evenly. 'That lady's as close as Boulder will ever come to having itself a glacier. There *is* one nice thing about her, though.'

'Her body?' Ellie guessed cynically. As far as she could tell, that was all the cowboy had been capable of noticing when he watched her broadcasts.

'Her voice,' he corrected. 'That lady has a voice like good aged Scotch going down smooth and easy on a winter night. I'll bet I could recognise it anywhere, even on a deserted road in the middle of the night.' He turned just enough to give her an impish smile. 'Why don't you try the ignition now, Eleanora?' he suggested. 'We'll get you off this mountain before you really do become an iceberg.'

'Oh.' He had known who she was from the beginning! From the first moment she had spoken, Ellie realised, meeting his grin with a low laugh of amusement at herself. He had been playing a game, but she was the one who had started it by pretending she didn't recognise him in the flashlight's glow. 'Thank you, Mr Kolter.'

She slid into the car and turned the key in the

ignition, breathing a sigh of relief when the engine spluttered into life.

'Let it run for a few minutes,' he suggested, slipping into the passenger side and shutting the door behind him. 'After you recharge the battery, I'll follow you into town just to make sure it doesn't stop again. Take it to your mechanic in the morning,' he continued, stripping off his gloves and blowing on his fingers to return the warmth. 'And, in the future . . .'

'Stay away from roads like this,' she predicted the lecture she was about to get. 'It was a short cut.'

'Did you save a lot of time?'

'No, but . . .'

'Look, lady,' he said evenly. 'It wouldn't take a lot of encouragement for a man to want a woman who looks like you. Half the men in Colorado already do.' Including him? she wondered, casting him a sidelong, curious glance, but his face was impassively stern. He was delivering a lecture to a dim-witted woman, not trying to romance her. For just a moment an irrational disappointment stirred inside her before relief took hold. 'You're the favourite subject on the local fantasy circuit right now,' he continued bluntly. 'A woman has to take care of herself in this world, because not every man is as decent as I am.'

That was an amusing statement, coming from the 'decent' man who had held her up to public ridicule, but he no doubt thought she had had it coming. She had stung him with her review before he had written his derisive song. But it wasn't exactly an even trade of insults. The review was over and done with in one night, but the song was still gaining popularity in Eastern Colorado—it was selling especially well wherever Eleanora Martin had a television audience.

'If you had been raped tonight, it would have been your own fault,' he went on relentlessly with the lecture. 'I don't care about all that women's equality garbage. When a woman has set herself up on the kind of pedestal you have, there are men who are going to dream of knocking her off.'

Oh, lord, Ellie thought impatiently, laying her head back against the car seat. The man was *that* type. If it were up to him, women would probably wear veils and never leave the house. 'If men are fantasising about me, it's because of your detestable song, not because of anything I've done,' she countered sharply. 'It's not fair that I have to go out of my way to avoid the trouble you've caused me.'

'Who told you that life is fair?' he demanded as he pulled out a cigarette and lit it with a quick thumbflick against his lighter. There was a long moment of cool silence before he added, 'Your review certainly wasn't.'

'You're not still angry about that, are you?' Doing reviews was part of her profession, and getting them was part of his. Besides, she hadn't been entirely negative. She had said that Kolter's voice was pleasantly expressive in the few songs that allowed him to explore a greater range. Apparently nothing short of abject adoration was good enough for him.

'I've had worse.'

'I'm sure you have.' She didn't realise what she'd said until his mouth twitched outward into a smile of mocking self-amusement. 'I didn't mean it that way,' she corrected quickly. 'I meant that . . . we're both professionals,' she faltered under the cynical amusement of his stare. 'And if you can't take criticism, then maybe you should . . .'

'How do you like the weather?'

'What?' His unexpected question stopped her in mid-sentence.

'I asked you how you like the weather,' he repeated as he rolled down the window and exhaled a sighing stream of smoke. 'My mother taught me to change the subject when a lady starts to stammer and to leave before I wear out my welcome. I thought I'd try one before I try the other.'

'Oh.' They weren't going to talk about the song or the review, Ellie understood, relieved that he had changed the subject before she had had a chance to make a complete fool of herself. For some reason she couldn't fully comprehend, that mattered to her with this man. 'It's freezing. I'd like the weather better if I were in a warm house with a cup of tea.'

'So would I,' he smiled. Then he cocked his head to listen to the engine. 'It sounds okay now,' he assessed the purring sound. 'My pickup doesn't do more than fifty-five, so don't be a hotshot when we get to the highway.'

With those last words he opened the car door and shut it again behind him. He had left before he'd worn out his welcome, she realised, watching him as he strode along the shoulder of the road and swung up into the truck with an easy self-assurance that she found unnervingly attractive. He'd left long before his welcome had worn out.

Ellie signalled for the last turn, glancing in her rear-view mirror to see if the two white globes of light would follow her now that she had reached the driveway of the Martin estate. She was pleased they did.

Because she wanted to thank him for helping her, Ellie told herself, trying to ignore the interest that had sparked too easily into life. The man was attractive. All right, she admitted impatiently to herself, the man was absolutely gorgeous. His face was square-jawed and tense, with a craggy remoteness to it that was strikingly at odds with the inviting laughter in his dark-eyed stare. It was as if he said, 'Come here,' in one breath, and 'But not too close,' in the very next. It was an intriguing combination, and no doubt one that many other women had remarked on.

He was a total stranger, Ellie reminded herself as she stopped her Lamborghini in front of the large white house that already sported a Christmas wreath on its broad oak door. No, they weren't total strangers. She had heard his music and he had watched her television broadcasts. That meant that they had met in that world where each of them existed as a public person. She knew him and he knew her, but they didn't know each other.

And that was probably for the best, she thought as she stepped out of her car and waited for the truck to stop behind her in the driveway. Given their public relationship so far, anything more could be an absolute disaster.

Still, he had helped her without a second thought, and she was grateful for everything except his condescending lecture. Which had turned into an argument, she reminded herself firmly. She'd thank the man and send him on his way. And that, she thought, was that. Until Ben Kolter ⁱ down from the truck and shut the door behind ⁱ.

'I'd rather have coffee than tea,' he volunteered, rubbing his gloved hands together in the chilly air. 'Can you manage that?'

'Yes,' she said, surprised. Had she offered him a cup of tea? She tried to remember exactly what she'd said, but he had already put his hand against her back in a not-quite-casual touch that coaxed her towards the house.

'You must make a nice living at the television station,' Kolter said as she unlocked the door and led him into a broad entrance foyer.

'It's my father's house.'

'Oh.' The man shoved his hands into his pockets with a frown. 'Do I have to go into the study and introduce myself to your father before I have a cup of coffee?'

'No.' The mail on the hall table was still unopened and there was no light on in the study to indicate her father's presence in the house. When he wasn't home this late, he was usually spending the night at his office or his club. 'He probably won't be home until tomorrow . . .' Ellie stopped herself, although she had already said too much. Her father wasn't expected home until the following evening. They were alone in the large house.

And that was exactly the question he had meant to ask, she realised, studying Ben Kolter's handsome face with wary disapproval. He was studying her as well, assessing her with an openness that put her on her guard. Then, suddenly, he smiled. '*Does* he own half of Colorado?' Kolter asked her curiously.

'Not quite half,' answered Ellie, put off by the bluntness of his question. Apparently his grasp of manners extended no farther than when to leave and when to change the subject. 'But he owns enough,' she added coolly. 'May I take your coat, Mr Kolter?'

She slid off her fur-edged coat and hung it in the hallway closet, then waited as he slipped out of his. She had expected him to seem much less powerful without the heavy sheepskin coat, but the shoulders underneath his cotton shirt were still broad and muscular, and he still moved with an easy, striding grace as if he owned everything he saw. Ellie wished she wasn't so aware of that.

'Is this you?' he asked, pausing beneath an oil portrait in the hallway. Catherine Martin sat straight-backed and regal in a wing-back chair with a pretty blonde-haired child beside her. The child was smiling bravely, but there was a lost and frightened quality to her green-eyed stare. That was the year her parents had decided to send her away to boarding school. With the

naïve innocence of youth, Ellie had thought the
fights between her parents were her fault, and
sending her away had proved that her fears were
true.

'Yes.' She answered the man's question. 'And
that was my mother. She died earlier this year.'

'She was a pretty lady,' Kolter said matter-of-
factly, returning his attention to the portrait.
'You look a lot like her.' He stared at the
painting, frowning as he studied the portrait of
the child, then he turned his back on it to meet
her eyes instead. His stare was far more than
simple curiosity, Ellie thought, catching her
breath as he reached out to touch her chin.
'What was the little girl afraid of?' he asked
unexpectedly.

So he had noticed that. Very few people did.
'I don't remember now,' she answered evasively,
unwilling to tell a stranger how badly she'd been
hurt by her parents' constant arguments. She
had been afraid of their anger and of their
silences, but most of all she'd been afraid of her
inability to stop them.

She had prayed for an end to their bitter
arguments, and when that end finally came it
brought a far worse situation. They simply
stopped caring about one another enough to
have a fight. Catherine Martin turned her energy
to collecting art and Ernest Martin collected
companies instead. 'I was afraid of everything
when I was twelve. Weren't you?'

'No.' His thumb edged up to stroke her cheek
with a touch that could have been accidental,
although Ellie had her doubts. 'When I was

twelve, I thought I was going to grow up to be Superman.'

'When did you realise you weren't?'

'What makes you think I'm not?' His touch was warmer now, and his eyes twinkled with amusement as he held Ellie's gaze.

Was he making a pass at her? Ellie wondered, taking a step back to ease her chin away from his softly caressing hand. There was a fine line between friendly curiosity and an invitation to far more, and this man seemed capable of walking it with a practised tread. 'Why don't you come into the kitchen?' she suggested evenly. 'You can have that cup of coffee before you leave.'

She didn't wait to hear his answer before she turned away and walked along the hallway, but she could hear his footsteps as he followed her into the spacious panelled kitchen. Ben Kolter sat down at the table and watched her as she measured coffee into a percolator on the counter. 'What do your friends call you?' he asked curiously, lighting a cigarette and blowing a long, sighing stream of smoke into the air. 'Nora?'

'Ellie.'

'Ellie,' he repeated. 'I like that.' She did, too, she realised as he said her name again, giving it an almost musical inflection. 'Ellies have pigtails and daisies in their hair,' he suggested fancifully. 'Bare feet . . . gingham dresses, and straw baskets filled with kittens——'

'I was supposed to have been an Elliott,' Ellie interrupted before he went further with the poetic fantasy that made her sound as if she belonged on the cover of a greeting card.

'Ah.' His eyes flickered down from her pretty, even-featured face, lingering just briefly on her shapely body before his lips stretched outward into an appreciatively warm smile. 'Somebody goofed.'

'So I've heard.' She hadn't meant to say that, nor had she meant the tone to be so harsh. Kolter's eyes came up with a curiosity that they weren't apt to lose until he'd heard an explanation. 'My mother's obstetrician was an expert on selecting the gender of a child,' she explained. 'I ruined his statistics.'

'Good,' he answered matter-of-factly. 'People shouldn't meddle with the mysteries of life.'

Ellie met his comment with a smile, although it wasn't a subject she enjoyed. There had been only one child in the Martin marriage, and it had been clear from the beginning that she wasn't the child that Ernest Martin had wanted. Maybe life would have been different for her parents if she had been a son. Her father would have had someone to carry on his name and the business empire he'd created.

Nothing more was said, and the silence bore down around them, making her uncomfortably aware of the clicking of the kitchen clock and the gurgling sounds that emanated from the percolator. But more than anything, she was aware of him. He leaned back in his chair and watched her with an interest he made no attempt to hide.

'It's finally ready,' she whispered with relief,

pouring out two cups of coffee and setting them on the table along with the cream and sugar bowl. 'It always seems to take longer when you're waiting.'

Ben Kolter sipped his coffee, but his eyes never left her melancholy face. 'You're prettier than you are on television,' he suggested finally. 'And taller. On my set you're only this high.' He held his hand six inches above the table. 'That was a pretty bad joke,' he admitted, drumming his fingers nervously against the table when she responded only with a feeble smile. 'This is a lot like having breakfast with a one-night stand, isn't it?'

'I wouldn't know,' Ellie answered, although she understood his nervousness. No matter how hard she tried to think of a subject, she couldn't come up with anything they might conceivably have in common. He was doing a lot better than she was at making small talk.

'You don't eat breakfast?'

'I don't have one-night stands.'

'Ah.' There was a wealth of unspoken information in that soft exhalation. 'That's too bad,' he added with a wryly quirking smile. 'That eliminates my next question.'

Ellie opened her mouth, then closed it again before she gave an answer. How was she supposed to respond to that? she wondered. It hadn't been her imagination after all. The invitation she had read in Ben Kolter's eyes was completely real. 'I don't even know you.'

'You could,' he answered bluntly. He shrugged

philosophically when she fixed him with a green-eyed, disapproving stare. 'There are a lot of women who'd faint if I said that to them.'

'Are there?' Ellie didn't try to disguise her amusement. The man certainly had an elevated opinion of his effect on women. 'Is that the way you prefer your women, Mr Kolter? Unconscious?'

His mouth stretched outward even farther, exposing a row of white, even teeth, then he laughed. It was an unexpectedly delighted laugh that Ellie found attractive despite her better sense. 'I like you, Ellie,' he admitted with every evidence of honesty. 'You're a class act. As a matter of fact,' he said, leaning forward as if he were about to confide a secret, 'I like you so much, I'm going to do you a favour. How would you like to appear on a nationally televised interview? Would that help your career?'

Ellie's coffee cup stopped half-way to her mouth and she stared at the man as if he were a little mad. 'Of course it would,' he answered his own question. 'You're in a profession where there are a thousand qualified reporters for every on-air job. And you're stuck here in Boulder where no one's ever going to see you. I can do something about that.'

What on earth did he think he could do? Ellie wondered. And for what price? She set down her coffee cup and met his eyes again. 'This isn't the old casting couch line, is it?' she asked suspiciously. 'Sleep with me and I'll make you a star?'

'You've heard that one, huh?'

'Yes,' she admitted honestly. She had had her share of propositions in the past, and she had always turned them down. What made this one so ludicrous was that Ben Kolter had absolutely nothing he could offer. Either he was crazy, or he thought that she might be.

'I'm going to give you the television exposure with no strings attached,' he offered generously. 'My band's doing an interview with the Nashville cable station. Why don't you appear with us?'

'With you?' Ellie was even more confused. Why would she appear on a television programme with the Travelling Asylum Band? And on a country music station?

'You're good at what you do, Ellie,' Kolter went on persuasively. 'You could be working in one of the major television markets. But unless you do something to call attention to yourself, you're going to grow old here in Boulder, Colorado, reviewing every two-bit ballet company and puppet show that comes along the pike. Think about it. This is national exposure. And national exposure could get you a better job.'

'What would *you* get out of it?' she asked suspiciously. She didn't for a minute think that Kolter was the kind of man who indulged in pointless charity.

'Isn't that obvious?' he shrugged. 'You don't think *Eleanora*'s been selling so well because it's a great song, do you?'

'Good heavens, no.'

'It's selling because of *you*, lady. Every woman in Colorado wants to be you. And every man in

Colorado wants to have you. You're the ice queen that every red-blooded man longs to melt.'

'Is that a compliment?'

'It could be,' he admitted, meeting her eyes with so much warm appreciation that Ellie glanced restlessly away. Did that apply to him as well? Did the attractive cowboy think he could melt her into submission with his seductive flattery? 'The song could be a compliment, too. Have you ever thought of that?'

'Is that why you wrote it?' Ellie challenged, meeting his stare at last. Only a mindless idiot would believe that Ben Kolter had written *Eleanora* as a tribute.

His mouth quirked outward at the edges, but this time it was his eyes that were the first to fall. 'Not exactly,' he admitted honestly. 'But you could pretend I did.'

'Right,' she answered unimpressed. 'And the British could pretend that they won the Revolutionary War. But it wouldn't change the facts.' And the facts were far more complicated than him simply doing her a favour.

He wanted her to help him promote his record. National exposure for her meant national exposure for *Eleanora*. If she sat sweetly by his side and discussed the record, what were people going to say? That a rowdy country cowboy had finally succeeded in melting the Boulder iceberg? That was lovely, Ellie thought cynically. That was just the image she wanted to have broadcast from coast to coast.

'You're the Lady, and I'm the Outlaw,' Kolter pressed a logic that obviously made more sense to him than it did to her. 'People want to see us together, Ellie. They want to see the excitement the two of us can generate when we're face to face. If we give the audience what they want, we get the attention we want, too. Everybody in show business plays this game.'

Hype. That was what Ben Kolter was proposing: an illusion with nothing real behind it, all designed to sell more copies of his records. 'I'm not your advertising gimmick, Mr Kolter,' she answered finally. 'And it's not in my interest to help you sell another copy of that insulting song.'

'We could be dynamite together, Ellie. Just think about . . .'

'No!'

He stopped and studied her stubborn face. Then he shrugged philosophically. 'Okay,' he agreed. 'I gave it my best shot, and you don't want to do it.' Despite his words, he didn't seem resigned, Ellie thought warily, noting the way his eyes darkened with a calculating hardness. He had lost the battle, but she sensed he hadn't given up the war. He leaned back in his chair and sipped his coffee.

'Would you like to have breakfast with me tomorrow morning?' he changed the subject once again. 'Breakfast, in this instance, meaning breakfast, nothing more.'

Breakfast, in this instance, meaning another chance to talk her into his ridiculous idea, Ellie thought, but that suspicion was dispelled the moment that it crossed her wary mind.

'We don't have to talk business,' Kolter added

in the silence. 'I like you, Ellie,' he admitted quietly. 'I'd like to see you again.'

And she wanted to see him again, she realised, but there was no future with this man. Except for the song that had thrown them together, there was absolutely nothing that they had in common.

'I can't. I'm sorry,' she apologised.

'Because you don't like me?'

'No. That's not it.' Oddly enough, she *did* like the man. He was irritatingly blunt and he was self-assured to the point of arrogance, but those faults were softened by a disarming ability to laugh at himself. When he met her eyes, she felt herself stir with a disquieting desire. No other man had ever made her feel quite so alive or as attractive as he did.

'Are you going to say that you don't like my music?'

'I don't,' Ellie admitted uncomfortably. 'But that's not the reason, either. I already have plans for tomorrow.'

'I see.' It was her turn, she understood. You could call me later in the week, or I'm free next Monday—either of those would have left him with some hope. But any hope was false, and Ellie steeled herself against the question in his eyes.

There was a physical attraction between them, but she was old enough to know that wouldn't take them far. Hopeless relationships were best ended before they had a chance to start. 'I see,' he repeated evenly, finishing his coffee, then getting up to put the empty cup beside the sink. 'I should be going.'

Even that was a question, and Ellie gave her answer by not answering at all. Instead, she followed him out of the kitchen and found his coat in the hall cupboard. 'Thank you for rescuing me, Mr Kolter,' she said as he slipped it on and buttoned it across his chest. 'I'll have my mechanic look at the car tomorrow.'

'You do that. And stay off those roads,' he cautioned as she opened up the door. He was half-way out of the door before he turned back again. 'The cable people are going to do the filming Friday afternoon at Sloan Murphy's ranch on Bendix Road. In case you change your mind.'

'I'll remember that,' she promised. 'But I won't change my mind.'

'I always stay with Murphy when I'm in Boulder,' he added quietly. His hand fell softly to her shoulder in a touch that sent an unexpected shock of excitement through her. 'His number's in the phone book. In case you change your mind.'

About seeing him again, Ellie understood as his fingers curled around her shoulder. In that one, silent moment she changed her mind a hundred times, but she pressed her lips together and refrained from blurting out an answer she'd regret when he had let her go and broken the spell of longing he could weave around her with his touch.

'Ellie . . .' Her breath stopped in her throat as he leaned down to kiss her, but his mouth brushed hers so softly that she had barely felt its warmth before he pulled away and smiled at her regretfully. 'Goodnight, lady.'

'Goodbye, Mr Kolter.' She watched as he backed down the stairs, then closed the door between them, wondering why she felt such a painful sense of regret for everything she hadn't done.

CHAPTER TWO

SLOAN MURPHY. Ellie saw the name on the mailbox at the side of Bendix Road and turned her Lamborghini into the long dirt driveway that snaked uphill to a weathered house.

It made no sense to come here, but she had thought of little else since the night Ben Kolter had said goodnight with a soft breath that had felt like a caress against her cheek. She had relived that last moment time and time again, remembering the tension in his shoulders as he rocked forward on the balls of his feet. He had wanted to kiss her more completely, Ellie knew, wishing now that she had had the courage to meet his eyes with an invitation to do exactly that.

But she had lost the moment, and he had gone. He had walked out of her life, but not out of her restless dreams. It made no sense at all to dream about the cowboy, but his face came back to her so vividly she could almost touch the craggy handsomeness of his taut cheeks and read the laughter in his deep brown eyes.

She had an old-fashioned schoolgirl infatuation, Ellie knew, embarrassed by how hard she had fallen for the last man on earth who should have appealed to her at all. He was a country singer,

31

down on his luck and struggling to regain the fame he'd once possessed, but she'd seen more than ambition in his eyes. There had been a self-possession that intrigued her and a hunger that stirred the blood inside her veins.

But more than anything, she'd been moved by something that he hadn't done. He hadn't once suggested that she should be grateful to him. He had stopped to help a total stranger, then he had followed her into Boulder to make sure her car wouldn't fail again. Without him, she might have spent a cold and terrifying night on a deserted highway, or she could have endured a far worse fate. But when he asked her to appear on the Nashville programme with his band, he hadn't suggested that she owed him a favour. It was up to her to realise that she did.

Ellie parked her car in the crowded driveway and got out to stride across the sere grasses of the lawn. No one answered her knock, so she turned the knob and let herself into the house. Music poured from a room farther down the hallway. It was *Eleanora*, she noted disapprovingly, separating Ben Kolter's clear baritone from the other voices as she made her way along the hallway, stepping carefully over the hookups for the cameras and audio equipment. She wished he had chosen any other song to sing.

'With eyes so green they shine like emeralds . . . The colour of an Arctic sea . . .' Ben caught sight of Ellie in the doorway and a delighted smile twitched upward at the edges of his lips, but he continued with the song. 'Hair like sunshine in the summer . . . Let it down and come to me . . .' His voice was so low and sensual it seemed like a private invitation to his arms.

'I watch the news for Eleanora . . . She won't tell me any lies . . .' She could take the song as a compliment, Ellie remembered Kolter's words as she listened to the rowdy chorus. Maybe she could see it as a compliment if she tried hard enough

'Let your hair down, Eleanora . . .' Kolter's voice was smooth as satin against her trembling nerves, and Ellie had to steel herself against the longing she could feel too easily for this seductive man. 'I don't mean you any harm . . . Come to me, my Eleanor . . . Become a woman in my arms . . .'

But it hadn't been written as a compliment, she reminded herself now. The man had a way of confusing everything she felt until white was no longer white and black no longer black. All the easy boundaries in her life melted like snow in a springtime thaw whenever he met her eyes with a dark-eyed stare that promised to prove every word he sang.

She didn't like his music, and the song had been written to ridicule her. But that didn't make them enemies, she had already decided. She could find some good things to say about the music and his band if she tried hard enough.

'Whoa!' One of the band members gave a shout to punctuate the ending of the song. Then he set down the guitar and peered at the camera that had been filming their performance. 'Is that thing still on?'

'Yes,' Eleanora spoke for the first time. 'Cameras are a lot like guns,' she volunteered, stepping forward as the members of the band turned to stare at her with blank surprise. Kolter hadn't told them she was coming, Ellie guessed. He couldn't have been sure of that himself, although he hadn't seemed surprised to see her. 'Always presume they're ready to shoot. If you don't, you're going to end up being wounded. Hello, Mr Kolter.' She held out her hand and Ben Kolter met it.

'Miss Martin,' he gave her a civil nod, but nothing could disguise the delighted sparkle in his eyes, 'I'm glad you decided to stop by.'

'I was in the neighbourhood,' she returned with equal dryness.

'Eleanora Martin,' he turned to include the band members in the conversation although he didn't loosen his warm grip on her hand, 'this is Trawler McKay, my drummer. G.T., my bass guitarist.'

'Pleased to meet you, ma'am,' responded G.T.

'And I'm Murphy.' The fourth member of the band stepped forward with his hand extended. 'I sing back-up. I don't know if you remember me from the concert.'

'Yes, of course I remember you.' Ellie had said that his inane antics underscored the witlessness of a mediocre band, but the man didn't seem to hold a grudge. Instead, his bright blue eyes sparkled with open friendliness when she gave him a shy smile.

'Fred Prentiss, the host of The *Country Music Hour*,' Ben continued with the introductions.

'Marty Tresh, the producer; John Reed, the cameraman. Marcie Donne's handling the audio equipment . . .' He introduced her to everyone involved. 'I told Marty and Fred that there was a chance you'd come, so they're all set to do an interview with just the two of us. Is that all right with you?'

'That's fine,' Ellie answered, somewhat unnerved by his lack of surprise. She hadn't known for certain that she'd be here until she had turned her Lamborghini up Sloan Murphy's driveway.

'Can we do the interview now?' Ben called to the producer above the pandemonium in the large room. 'Miss Martin's a busy woman. I don't think we should take too much of her time.'

The producer agreed, and a few minutes later Ellie was sitting on a couch in Sloan Murphy's living-room facing the handsome singer across a coffee table that had been hurriedly cleaned off. Fred Prentiss slid into an easy chair that had been positioned behind the table and tapped on the microphone that was attached to his lapel. 'Are we okay with the sound?'

'Okay!' a disembodied voice called back. 'I'll cue you for the end of the intro.'

'We just have to sit here for a minute,' the ruddy-faced man explained. 'We've got to have a visual for the opening credits.'

'I understand what we're doing, Mr Prentiss,' Ellie reassured him. The film that was being shot now would appear without their voices, a

backdrop for the opening theme and credits of
the *Country Music Hour* .

'Ellie's a real pro,' Ben interjected proudly.
'Her reviews are the only thing worth watching
on the Boulder channel.'

'Why, thank you, sir.' She smiled, meeting his
warm eyes and losing herself for a long moment
there. She was glad that she had changed her
mind about the interview. There was no reason
to be enemies, she decided, noting the way his
mouth quirked outward into an inviting smile
that touched her like a smooth, caressing hand.
She could find something good to say about his
music if she tried.

'You're on, Fred,' the producer called. Fred
looked straight ahead, giving a broad smile for
the benefit of the camera.

'Howdy, folks. This is Fred Prentiss and the
Country Music Hour . We've got a real treat for
all you music fans today. We're out here in
Boulder, Colorado, with Ben Kolter, who is
making a comeback from a ten-year retirement.
And we're also talking to Eleanora Martin, the
entertainment reporter for the local TV station
they've got out here. Let me start by asking you
your opinion of the Travelling Asylum Band,
Eleanora. Are they any good?'

'I think they're as good as any country music
band.' She could say that, at least, with total
honesty. She didn't like any country music.

'You like their music?' the host asked, distinctly
disappointed. 'What about their latest release,
Eleanora?'

'*Eleanora* is . . . lively,' Ellie answered,

pausing only a brief momemt to select a word
that might lay within the realm of truth.

'Lively?' Fred Prentiss frowned and cast a
worried glance at Ben, who stared intently at
the tip of his brown leather boot. 'You say you
like Ben Kolter's music, and yet the review you
gave the Travelling Asylum Band . . . Well, let
me quote from it directly. I've got it somewhere
here . . .' He paused to find a paper on the
table in front of him and then he read, '"Most
of Kolter's music fits into the My-baby-left-me-
and-the-cat-is-drunk category of country primitive. The fans who have been waiting ten
years for this man to return will be woefully
disappointed by his repetitious melodies and his
unsophisticated lyrics." That's pretty straight to
the gut.' Fred Prentiss gave a whistle. 'Is this
what started your famous feud with Ben Kolter?'

The feud was *famous* now? Or would it help
the ratings the *Country Music Hour* to pretend it
was? That was far more likely, Ellie knew, trying
to control her growing distaste for the host. He
had already decided on his version of the truth,
and he was going to ask leading questions until
he got the version that he wanted. It was up to
her to steer clear of all the traps he set.

'If you read the transcript of the review more
carefully, you'll find that I had some positive
things to say about Mr Kolter and his music,'
she countered evenly. 'As for our reported feud,
that's nothing but a media invention. There are
no hard feelings between Mr Kolter and myself.
He's professional enough to take criticism, and I
can certainly take a joke.'

Ben met her eyes with a troubled frown. 'That's it?' Fred Prentiss asked with overt disappointment. 'There is *no* feud between you and the Travelling Asylum Band?'

'The feud's just a piece of gossip,' Ben came to her rescue. Then his eyes dropped restlessly away, and Ellie was filled with an irrational foreboding. 'It's no closer to the truth than any of the other things people say about Eleanora Martin.'

What other things? Ellie wondered, staring at him with wary disbelief.

'Other things?' Fred Prentiss prompted hopefully, turning now to Ben. 'What other things do people say?'

'Oh . . . That she got her job because her daddy owns the television station.'

Her father didn't own the television station! He was a stockholder in the corporation that owned the building, nothing more.

'And I don't believe she slept her way into it, either. That's just another rumour,' Ben went on relentlessly, meeting her stunned eyes at last. 'I think the lady got the job because she's got old-fashioned moxie. She doesn't know the first thing about music, but that doesn't stop her from telling every man, woman and child in Colorado what entertainment is worth a damn and what isn't. I've got to admit it, I admire the lady's *chutzpah*.'

Ellie was flabbergasted by the man's audacity. He was ridiculing her! He was ripping her up one side and down the other on a nationally

broadcast television programme after she had
come here to do him a favour!

No, she corrected herself. She hadn't come
just to do the man a favour. She had come here
because she was already half in love with him
and was willing to feel more. She had innocently
presumed that he had some feeling for her, too.
But a man who was willing to ridicule her
publicly couldn't have felt anything at all.

Ellie met his eyes with a frosty stare. 'I have
the credentials to be an entertainment critic, Mr
Kolter.'

'I know you do,' he reassured her evenly. 'I
wrote a song about them. Remember?'

Her looks? That was all he thought it took to
be a television journalist? What had happened
to all the praise he'd given her when he was
trying to convince her to do the interview? He'd
said that she had enough talent to be successful
in a major television market. Now he was telling
everybody in the country that she was laughably
inept?

The man was a sleazy, rotten snake, and the
minute she was alone with him she'd tell him
exactly what she thought. But not now. Ellie
forced herself to stay in control of her rising
fury. Right now they were being filmed, and she
wouldn't give him the satisfaction of making a
complete fool of her in front of a television
audience.

'And I don't believe that she's an iceberg, like
everybody claims,' Ben Kolter went on, baiting
Ellie mercilessly. 'Maybe she looks like one, all
dressed up in her expensive blue suit with a

string of pearls at her throat, but I have a theory about her.'

'I'm sure you do, Mr Kolter.' Ellie's voice had fallen to a low, hoarse murmur that was meant to be a warning. If he persisted with this nonsense she'd fight back. 'Some men have theories about everything they don't understand.'

'I think the lady acts so cold and distant because she's afraid of men. I think she used her review to attack me because she's afraid of what men like me can make her feel. Is that your problem, Eleanora?'

'No, Mr Kolter,' Ellie disagreed. 'I'm not the one who has a problem. If you remember, I praised the way you sang a few of . . .'

'"The Travelling Asylum Band employs theatrics to stretch the limits of a musically impoverished programme"?' Ben Kolter quoted her own words. 'Is that your idea of praise?'

'No,' she answered icily, even more infuriated by his interruption. 'It's my idea of truth.'

'Musically *impoverished?*' he repeated irritably. 'How can you attack something you know nothing about? Have *you* ever written music?'

'One doesn't have to be a hen to know the eggs are bad,' she pointed out, meeting his stare with haughty coolness. 'The truth is that you were unprepared for that concert. You used old material. The new material you did use was inadequately rehearsed, and you tried to excuse your mistakes by telling the audience that the concert was a trial run for the newly re-assembled band.' His mouth tightened into an irritated line, but he didn't disagree with her assessment of the concert. He knew that it was true.

'I don't get paid to excuse your mistakes,' she pressed the point. 'I get paid to report them. And that's exactly what I did.'

She had won the round, she thought, leaning back in her chair as if the subject had been closed. But she hadn't counted on Ben Kolter's infinite resourcefulness. He sat back, too, and regarded her with a wounded sadness. 'You're right. We weren't ready for that concert,' he surprised her by admitting. 'I agreed to do it because I wanted to meet you.'

What was he doing now? she wondered, meeting his eyes with a plea to stop this nightmare before it escalated any further.

'I've been watching you for a long time on the television, Eleanora, and I guess . . . Well, I guess I got caught up in my own fantasy,' he apologised with just a shade too much shy hesitation for Ellie to believe. 'I thought you'd give us a good review. Then I'd go by the television station to thank you, and one thing would lead to another. When that didn't happen, I wrote the song. It was my tribute to the beautiful lady I couldn't get out of my mind. I never meant to hurt you,' he assured her, leaning forward in his seat to talk to her alone. To her, Ellie thought cynically, and to all the wide-eyed viewers who would be witnessing this fabricated scene. 'All I ever wanted was to be alone with you for just a little while.

'I wanted to take that pretty yellow hair down,' Ben continued softly. 'I wanted to smooth it across your shoulders with my fingers, and then I wanted to kiss you. Nice and slow so I wouldn't scare you right at first.'

His eyes never left her face, and his voice vibrated with a sensual promise that excited her despite her resolve to hold herself aloof. And it would be exciting the imaginations of everyone who watched this film, Ellie knew, calculating the effects of his suggestions. The man knew how to handle himself in front of a camera. She was sure of that.

And he knew how to handle himself with women. His sympathetic interest in her life, his hesitation at her door, even his suggestion that she use his interview on the Nashville station to further her career, were all designed to win her confidence so he could lure her into this trap. He had intended to fabricate a feud in order to sell his records, and he was going to do it whether she co-operated with him or not.

'I'd go real easy with you, Eleanora,' Ben promised quietly. 'I'd treat you like the wild, frightened creature that I know you really are. I'd be so gentle and so careful that you'd come to trust me. You'd let me touch you and you'd welcome the pleasure I could make you feel. That's what I dreamed of when I watched you on the television.

'I want to be good to you, Eleanora,' he continued his deliberately seductive charade. 'Do you know what I'd do after we'd made love?'

For a moment she was frightened by the sensual promise in his eyes, and she wondered if Ben Kolter knew this was an act. The question hung in the air between them for a long moment until Ellie regained enough composure to give him an icy smile. 'I hope you wouldn't sing,' she snapped sarcastically, noting the way Ben's lips twitched outward imperceptibly at her tart response.

'You *don't* like Kolter's music?' Fred Prentiss leapt into the fray and Ellie turned her cold green eyes on him. All he wanted was a piece of film that would make his ratings climb. He was no better than Ben Kolter.

'No. But that's the least of what I dislike about this man.' She smiled coldly as she got to her feet. 'The interview is over, Mr Prentiss.' With that she turned on her heels and stalked away, grabbing her coat as she strode through the hallway to the door.

'What the hell were you doing in there?' The last words she heard were delivered in a gravelly mutter that she identified as Sloan Murphy's voice, then she slammed the door behind her and stalked resolutely to her car. How could she have been attracted to a man like Kolter? He wanted publicity and nothing more. Hype! Ellie thought as she opened the door of her Lamborghini and tossed the coat inside. He didn't have enough faith in his own talent to make it honestly. He had to invent a gimmick to help him sell his songs. Well, Eleanora Martin was no one's advertising gimmick!

'Ellie!' The door slammed shut again and she heard footsteps pursuing her but she didn't turn around. 'You were terrific!' Kolter said, catching her arm to stop her. 'I was worried for a minute, but I knew that if I made you mad enough you'd come back like a she-wolf closing for the kill. You and I make a wonderful team, love. Marty said we generated enough electricity to light up everything this side of the Mississippi River.'

'Team?' she demanded, giving him a sarcastic stare. 'You suggested that I'm an incompetent reporter who got her job by handing out sexual favours. Or am I mistaken about your wretched little innuendoes?'

'What did you want me to say? You were dying in there with your polite little chit-chat about professionalism and being able to take a joke. No one was going to watch an interview like that. But now . . .' He reached up to cup her chin with an appreciatively warm hand. 'Do you know how magnificent you were, lady? You levelled me with that green-eyed stare of yours, and you cut the outlaw down to size. That's going to play like first-class theatre.'

He thought she had been acting? Ellie met his eyes with so much incredulous bewilderment that Kolter smiled. 'Fred Prentiss didn't want to air a show about a has-been band,' he confided honestly. 'But now he's changed his mind.'

'Fred Prentiss is a piece of slime.' Ellie jerked her arm to remove it from Kolter's grip, but he still held it firmly.

'Maybe he is,' he readily agreed. 'But he can get us national exposure. *Us*, love,' he repeated pointedly. 'I thought you understood how the interview was going to go. You're the Ice Queen and I'm the country cowboy. People don't want to see us chatting politely about music. Now that *Eleanora* has made it to the charts, we could write our own tickets as long as we have the sense to give people what they . . .'

'Charts?' Ellie stared at him, appalled. '*Eleanora* has made the *national* country music charts? It's being sold from coast to coast?'

'From Baltimore to Santa Fe,' he informed her proudly. 'I'm going to be back on top again, and I'm going to take you with me, Ellie.'

The national charts? Ellie felt dazed and numb as Ben Kolter ran his thumb seductively across her hand. That smutty little song was being played from one coast to the other. She was being ridiculed from Boston to L.A!

'Think about it, Ellie. A television executive in New York City is going to hear that song on the radio, and he's going to ask, "Who's Eleanora?" He's going to be curious enough to tune in to station WQBX. And then you've got it made, love. When the rest of the country gets a look at you, they'll be beating down your door. I'm doing you a favour, and some day you're going to see that.'

Did he honestly believe that? Ellie wondered. He was making a fool of her, and any television station that would hire her on the basis of that song wouldn't be looking for a serious reporter. What kind of a career would she be left with once the publicity had worn thin?

'I wasn't born yesterday,' she snapped, pulling her arm away from his. 'You're making a fool of me in order to promote your record. And I'm not going to allow it.'

'What can you do about it?' Kolter challenged, undeterred by Ellie's fury. 'Are you going to complain about me to your viewers?'

She stopped in her tracks and met his eyes with a cold anger that went deeper than anything she'd ever felt before. He had gained her confidence and then betrayed it. He had made a fool of her, and he had every intention of continuing. But it was his derision that stung her most of all. Did the man think he was so powerful she couldn't fight him?

'No, Mr Kolter. I'm not going to give you any free air time. I'm going to get myself a lawyer and slap an injunction on that song.' She had hit him where he was capable of being hurt. For just a moment his face darkened with a cloud of doubt. 'I'm going to claim that it holds me up to public ridicule and thereby infringes on my right to earn a living.'

'You can't stop that song.'

'Maybe not,' she answered, sliding into her car and turning the key in the ignition. 'But I can slow it down.'

Ben Kolter didn't answer. He stood at the side of the driveway with his hands shoved deeply into his pockets, watching her in moody silence as she backed out and headed for the highway.

CHAPTER THREE

IT WAS unusual for Ernest Martin to be home at all. He was always at his office or on a business trip, and even when he was home, he usually took his meals in the study while he pored over business contracts. But tonight was different. He had left Ellie a note that they were going to have a very special dinner guest and he wanted her to be there.

It was Rachel Wonson, Ellie guessed, sorting through her jewellery box until she found a pair of small gold earrings that went perfectly with her beige-coloured dress. He had instructed the cook to make Beef Wellington and her special orange soufflé for dessert. And, quite uncharacteristically for Ernest Martin, he had ordered flowers for the table.

Rachel Wonson was the widow of his former business partner. Her parents had known the Wonsons for close to twenty years, and Ellie had always liked the reserved and graceful white-haired woman. 'Why don't I call Mrs Wonson and suggest that we make a threesome?' she had suggested more than once when she had been given extra tickets to a performance she thought the woman might enjoy. Her father had always pleaded business, although Ellie had an intuition

that he had called her on his own. Lately he'd
seemed happier than he had been in years.

She put on her earrings and checked her
make-up one last time in the dresser mirror. He
would be in the study having an aperitif, she
knew, descending the curved stairway to the
hallway and turning right. But when she pushed
open the door she was surprised. No one was
there except her father's secretary.

'Miss MacDonald?' Ellie greeted her. 'Does
my father know you're here?'

'Yes. Someone came to the door right after I
did, so your father told me to wait in here until
he was free. I hope that's all right with you.'

'Of course it is,' answered Ellie reassuringly as
she crossed to the sideboard bar and took out a
glass. Poor Sara-Jean, she thought sympath-
etically. She worked with Ernest Martin all day
long, and now he had her running errands for
him on her spare time, too. He worked morning,
noon, and night, and he saw nothing odd in
asking his employees to do the same. 'Let me
pour you something to drink,' Ellie offered,
remembering her manners and taking out a
second glass. 'A sherry?'

'Yes.' Sara-Jean was grateful. 'You have a
beautiful house. The house I grew up in was
about one-tenth this size. And there weren't any
nice antiques, although my mother did everything
she could to make it look nice. Your mother
did, too,' she rambled nervously. 'I can tell just
by looking around that she cared about pretty
things.'

'She did,' Ellie agreed, studying Sara-Jean's

flushed face. The woman was Ellie's age, with dark hair that outlined a pretty, friendly face. There was nothing outstanding in her features, but the sum total of the neatly combed short hair, brown eyes and patiently set mouth was usually one of quiet pleasantness. Here in the Martin house, surrounded by the expensive artwork and antiques that Catherine Martin had collected, Sara-Jean seemed nervous and ill at ease.

'Was it an older woman who came to the door?' Ellie changed the subject as she gestured to a chair. 'A tall woman with beautiful white hair?'

'No, it was a man. A young man, I think,' Sara-Jean admitted. 'I didn't see him, but I could hear his voice for just a minute. Is something wrong?' she asked when Ellie wrinkled up her nose.

'We're supposed to have a very special dinner guest tonight. If it's a young man, that means my father's trying to fix me up with some investment banker he's discovered.' Ellie was distinctly disappointed. It would have done her father good to forget business for a while and see Rachel Wonson. 'No wonder he was so secretive about it. If he had told me he was matchmaking, I probably would have found a way to miss it.'

'Oh . . .' Sara-Jean seemed more uncomfortable than ever. 'It's a surprise, then? The identity of this dinner guest?'

'Until it turns into a shock,' Ellie answered with a laugh. 'My father's idea of what kind of man appeals to me is sometimes rather wide of the mark. I suppose you have the same kind of problem with your father.'

'I wish he was still around to worry about me like that,' Sara-Jean answered honestly. 'Both of my parents are gone now.'

'Oh, I'm sorry.' Then, because Sara-Jean didn't seem the type to be offended, Ellie gave her a mischievous smile. 'Would you like my banker?'

'What?'

'I'm serious,' Ellie answered as she sipped her sherry. 'Stay for supper and meet this man. Maybe you'll like the type.'

'I should think a banker would be more your type than mine,' Sara-Jean demurred. 'I wouldn't know what to say to him.'

'If you can carry on a conversation with my father, you can carry on a conversation with anyone,' Ellie reassured her, although she couldn't deny the truth of what Sara-Jean had said. A banker should have been her type. Instead, it was a country singer who had got under her skin to drive her crazy with a mixture of fury and desire.

'Besides . . .' Sara-Jean stared down into her glass as if the pale yellow liquid held the answers to life's mysteries, 'I'm already . . . involved.'

'Oh?' Ellie was intrigued by her troubled reticence. 'With someone from the office?'

'Yes.' Sara-Jean inhaled a breath as if to give her courage. 'I'm surprised your father hasn't told you about it.'

'My father doesn't gossip about anyone from

the office. As a matter of fact, we have such different schedules, we hardly see each other. This man . . .' Ellie frowned, wondering why Sara-Jean seemed so eager to confide in her and yet so terribly uncomfortable with what she had to say. 'He's not married, is he?'

'Oh, no,' the woman reassured her quickly. 'That's not the problem. That's the only thing that *isn't* a problem,' she added with an unhappy shrug. 'We're so totally different that I don't know how I'm going to fit in with his friends or his family.'

'Do you love him?'

'With all my heart,' Sara-Jean responded. 'I've loved him for a long time without knowing that he loved me, too. Then everything happened at once, and now he wants more than I think we should . . .' Sara-Jean didn't have a chance to finish before the study door swung open. The woman glanced up with an embarrassed start.

'I've invited your over-worked secretary to supper,' Ellie announced to cover any embarrassment Sara-Jean might feel as her father stepped into the room. Her glance defied her father to object, but he surprised her.

'What a wonderful idea,' he laughed. 'Will you stay for supper, darling?'

Time stood still for a long moment in which Ellie saw everything in painfully defined detail. Ernest Martin was a handsome man, endowed by nature with the kind of constitution that seemed immune to ageing. He was ramrod straight and trim, and the only sign of his sixty years was a head of snow white hair that only

served to make him look distinguished. But his
finest feature was a pair of finely manicured,
expressive hands, and one of those now rested
possessively against Sara-Jean's slim shoulder.

Sara-Jean had been talking about her father.
He was sixty, and she was less than half his age!
For a moment Ellie was too shocked to speak,
but her next reaction was a cynical disappointment
in Sara-Jean. She was a common, ordinary
fortune-hunter. And her halting little speech
about love had been intended to win Ellie's
sympathy for their ludicrous affair.

'You didn't tell your daughter about us.' Sara-
Jean's comment stopped just short of being an
accusation, but she softened it with a shy smile
at the man beside her.

'I wanted her to meet you first,' Ernest Martin
said, oblivious to the frown that creased the
corners of his daughter's mouth. 'I knew that
once you had a chance to talk you'd find that
you have a lot in common.'

'We should,' Ellie pointed out, taking a long
swallow of her sherry to fortify her nerves for
the evening that lay ahead. 'We're the same
age.'

Her father didn't seem to get the point of her
sharp-tongued comment, but Sara-Jean was bright
enough to recognise it as an insult. Her brown
eyes met Ellie's with a surprise that solidified
into a wary anger, but she didn't answer her in
kind. Sara-Jean was much too shrewd to show
her wealthy lover what kind of woman she could
be.

It wasn't hard to guess what had happened.

After her mother's death her father had spent even more time than ever at his office, completely absorbed in the world of contracts and interest rates. Sara-Jean would have been there at his side, patient and helpful, pretending to an interest in everything he did. She only had to wait for a moment when the loneliness of a widower grew great enough for him to turn to the woman most readily at hand. If she had seemed reluctant to ask for anything beyond the moment's unexpected passion, so much the better. Ernest Martin would have taken that as evidence of her sincerity.

'I have a surprise,' her father announced, rubbing his long-fingered hands together in a gleeful gesture that only served to make Sara-Jean more uncomfortable than she had been before.

'I don't think this is a good night for surprises, Ernie. Ellie looks . . . tired,' she suggested for lack of any better word.

Ellie could think of a more accurate word without a bit of effort. She was furious! How dared her father bring his lover here and expect her to be polite? Next he'd take her to his country club and set the entire state buzzing with derisive gossip.

'This surprise is for *you*, Sara-Jean,' he answered with a delighted laugh. 'Come into the dining-room, both of you.' He still held his arm around Sara-Jean's slim shoulders, but his free hand reached out to coax Ellie along with them to the other room.

'I trust we haven't kept you waiting too long?'

he spoke to the man who stood in front of the dining-room fireplace examining the Pittman landscape that hung above the mantel.

'I'm an old hand at waiting.' He smiled as he turned around and met two pairs of startled eyes. Ellie's surprise was mixed with shock and the suspicion that she had somehow slipped into a nightmare that wouldn't end even if she tried to shake herself awake. But Sara-Jean's reaction was far more pure and innocent.

'Ben Kolter!' She held out her hand. 'I've been listening to your records since I was a teenager. You're my favourite singer!'

'Mr Martin told me that,' admitted Ben as he reached out to meet her hand. 'I came to return his daughter's tool-kit and he invited me to stay for supper. I hope the invitation still stands.' He cast only the briefest glance at Ellie's disapproving face before his mouth curved upward into a boyishly warm smile. 'I've been standing here inhaling the aromas from the kitchen, and I don't think you could get me out of here without a slice of whatever that heavenly creation is.'

'I'll have to tell the cook you said that,' Ernest laughed. 'My name is Ernie, by the way. This is Sara-Jean, and you've already met my daughter, Ellie. Or Eleanora, as she's better known in Boulder.'

Ben's eyes flickered to Ellie's face. 'Yes, sir,' he agreed, catching Ellie's hand before she had a chance to pull away. 'I've had the pleasure of meeting both Ellie and Eleanora. And both of them are beautiful.' With that he bent and brushed her knuckles with his lips in a courtly gesture that was a bit too exaggerated for Ellie to take seriously. He was making fun of her, but it was subtle enough to fool everyone but her.

'Thank you for returning my tool-kit, Mr Kolter.' She slipped her hand away from his. 'You've been smelling the Beef Wellington. Why don't we sit down and eat it?' And get this ungodly meal over with, she thought, although she kept her bitter sentiment to herself. It was bad enough to have a social-climbing gold-digger at their table, without having to endure the derision of a shiftless singing cowboy, too. But Sara-Jean seemed absolutely delighted by the unexpected turn of events. And what delighted Sara-Jean delighted Ernest Martin. He was so smitten by his girlfriend that he could barely take his eyes away from her tremulously smiling face.

They sat, her father at one end of the table and Sara-Jean at the other. Where her mother used to sit, Ellie noted, wondering if her father had any idea how she felt about the situation, or whether he was so enamoured of his pretty secretary that he couldn't think of anything but her. Ellie sat across the table from Ben Kolter, maintaining a stiff and disapproving silence through which Sara-Jean's excited words tumbled on and on.

Sara-Jean was a storehouse of Ben Kolter information. She could name his albums and all the songs, in precise order, on every side. She could quote whole verses of inanities about waitresses with hearts of gold and love-sick desperadoes. And Ben Kolter, with his pulsating, throbbing ego, enjoyed every fawning word.

They deserved each other, Ellie thought, picking at her meat with little appetite.

'Tell me . . .' Ben leaned over to speak to Sara-Jean, 'what do think of my new song?'

'*Eleanora*?' Sara-Jean hesitated, casting a wary glance at Ellie and then at Ernest Martin. 'I don't really know,' she answered carefully. 'I've only heard it once or twice.'

'I like it,' Ernest answered for her. 'It's got a lively melody.' Ellie gave him an incredulously harsh stare. Her father liked the smutty little piece of music that mentally undressed his daughter? 'It's a compliment, isn't it?'

'Yes, sir,' admitted Ben as he leaned back in his chair and stared across the table, but Ellie refused to meet his eyes. 'It surely is.'

What a liar the man was! What an unmitigated, arrogant, filthy, deceiving liar! Ellie took a breath to stop the retort she almost made in fury. The man had ridiculed her publicly, but she certainly wasn't going to give him the pleasure of goading her into another explosion of ill temper. Eleanora Martin had nerves that were every bit as firm as his. She met his brown eyes with a level, green-eyed stare of challenge, but they didn't waver under the cold iciness of hers.

'Maybe you'd be willing to write a song for Sara-Jean,' suggested Ernest as he stood up to retrieve a brandy bottle from the sideboard bar. Their best brandy, Ellie noted. The 1904 Armagnac that her father only served to his most honoured guests. 'I'd pay you well for it. It would be a wedding present from me to Sara-Jean.'

Ellie's coffee cup stopped half-way to her lips, only briefly, but it was enough for Ben to note. His attention flickered from her taut, angry mouth to Sara-Jean's evasively restless eyes before he answered. 'I don't usually write songs for other people,' he demurred. 'I write them for myself.'

'We haven't decided to get married,' said Sara-Jean weakly. Ellie stared straight ahead, concentrating on a spot of gravy that had stained the tablecloth just a few inches from Ben Kolter's plate. He wouldn't marry his secretary? Not now? Not just ten months after Catherine Martin had been laid to rest? And *her*, of all people! A nobody from the mountains of Colorado who had absolutely nothing to offer him except the pleasures of her body.

In time that pleasure would grow thin and he would find himself trapped in a marriage that would prove even unhappier than his first one had been. But Ellie knew her father wouldn't listen if she tried to tell him that. He was an old man caught up in the headiness of love the second time around.

'*I've* decided to get married,' Ernest disagreed, setting a glass of brandy beside Ben's plate. 'And I don't intend to take no for an answer. What do you think I should do, Ben? Kidnap her and drag her up into the mountains until she agrees to be my wife?'

'That would be one way,' Ben agreed, taking

a thoughtful sip of his drink. His eyes lingered on Ellie's face, watching her so closely she could barely breathe under the curiosity of his stare. He could read every bitter thought that passed through her chaotically troubled mind. If a total stranger could do that, why couldn't her father understand the pain his words were causing?

'Sara-Jean wanted us to keep our relationship a secret until we were sure of how we felt,' admitted Ernest. He set a glass of brandy beside Ellie and Sara-Jean and returned to the sideboard to pour one for himself. 'But I've been sure from the beginning. I've been a gold-plated fool most of my life, Ben. I had nothing when I started, and I've worked hard all of my life to make something of myself. I've been so busy making money I've never understood that the most important thing in life is love. Sara-Jean has made me see how empty my life has always been. Well, that emptiness is over,' he said firmly, letting his hand fall affectionately to her shoulder. 'I'm going to marry this woman. And I'm going to have a child.'

Ellie's stomach twisted with a primitive jealousy. What did her father think *she* was? Just because he had been too busy to pay any attention while she was growing up it didn't mean she wasn't his child, too.

'Ernie, honey . . .' Sara-Jean patted his hand in a feeble gesture, but he didn't take the hint.

'Sara-Jean thinks there will be gossip about the difference in our ages,' he said candidly. 'I'm sixty years old.'

'I suppose there *will* be gossip,' Ben agreed

matter-of-factly. 'Where I come from there's a word for men who marry women like Sara-Jean.' His mouth quirked upward at the corners as he glanced at the flustered woman. 'The word is lucky.'

The word was crazy, Ellie thought, but she sipped her brandy in sullen silence. She knew her father well enough to know that he'd do exactly what he wanted. He always had. Maybe that ruthless self-interest had been the reason for his business success, but it hadn't made his wife happy. And now he was showing the same callous disregard for his daughter's feelings. Only Sara-Jean seemed aware of Ellie's bleak unhappiness, and Ellie refused to meet her regretfully sad eyes.

'Maybe I *will* write a song for you,' Ben offered when Ernest took his place again at the table. 'But, if I do, it won't be for money. It will be repayment for your hospitality.' His eyes brushed Ellie's for a second before he raised his glass in a toast to Sara-Jean. 'And a tribute to the power of love the second time a man is blessed with that kind of miracle.'

'Please excuse me.' Ellie was on her feet before she realised what she was doing. She had to get away from all of them. If she didn't, she was going to scream. 'I have work to do. Thank you for returning my tool-kit, Mr Kolter.' She didn't wait for a response before she turned abruptly and left the room.

They were two of a kind! she thought, furious at Sara-Jean for weaving a spell that trapped a foolish old man into a ludicrous marriage and furious at Ben Kolter for encouraging the idiocy even further. He liked Sara-Jean because she was a fawning little groupie incapable of telling the difference between real music and the kind of caterwauling noise his band produced.

Well, let them have each other! she decided. They could linger over their brandies while Sara-Jean stoked the fires of his pulsating ego. Eleanora Martin certainly wasn't going to do that for him, nor for any man!

CHAPTER FOUR

THEY deserved each other, Ellie thought, opening her cupboard to find a pair of riding trousers and a cashmere sweater. Sara-Jean was nothing but a scheming fortune-hunter who had managed to get a hold on a foolish old man. And Ben Kolter . . . Well, he'd already proved what kind of man he was. He was a liar and a con man who wasn't above using unsuspecting women if he could gain advantage for himself.

Ellie changed into her riding clothes, then slipped down the back stairway and out of the door. Ben Kolter's truck was still parked in the driveway, and she passed it without a second glance, striding through the crystal sharpness of the night towards the only place on earth she knew would drain away her anger.

She inhaled the comforting aroma of hay and horses as she stepped into the stables and switched on the electric lights. This was her favourite world, far removed from the glamour of the television studio and the empty affluence of her father's house. This was the place she had always run to when she was filled with misery and anger, and it had never failed to give her strength. 'There's a beautiful moon out there, Reggie.' Ellie spoke as she approached her

favourite gelding and reached up to stroke his
satiny smooth nose. 'Let's ride all the way to the
edge of the universe tonight.' The horse
responded with a low whinny of appreciation as
he nudged her arm.

'That's a long ride to make alone,' a low voice
responded. Ellie let out a startled cry as Ben
Kolter's hand fell softly to her shoulder, but his
fingers curled to hold her still before she could
pull away. 'Where do you suppose the edge of
the universe is, Ellie?'

'According to my father, the universe begins
and ends with Sara-Jean.'

'Ah.' His voice vibrated with an amused
understanding as his finger reached up to lightly
tease her ear. 'And what about *your* universe,
pretty lady? Does it have room for someone
other than your daddy?'

He was making fun of her, and this time Ellie
wasn't amused by his sardonic humour. 'You
don't know what's going on,' she snapped as she
shook his hand away and stalked into the tack
room to find a saddle for Sir Reginald.

'How much bigger does the writing on the
wall have to get before you think that I can read
it?' Kolter disagreed. 'You don't mind being
adored by the peasants, but God forbid your
daddy should marry one.'

'She's after his money.'

'What if she is?' he asked her evenly. 'Any
woman who marries your father is going to earn
her keep. Not that I didn't like the old man,'
Ben added quickly when Ellie looked up to fix
him with an icy stare. 'But he's obviously the

type who thinks women were put on earth to make him happy.'

'And you aren't that type?'

'No ma'am.' His grin was far too quick. 'I was put on earth to make women happy. I keep offering to prove that to you.'

'I'm sure you'd like to try, Mr Kolter,' Ellie snapped an irritable rejoinder to his less-than-subtle proposition. 'But I'm not interested in a man like you.'

'You were yesterday,' he reminded her, reaching up to stroke a chestnut roan. 'Before I was stupid enough to mess things up. Can I ride this one?' he changed the subject before she could respond. 'I like her big brown eyes.'

'No. You may *not* ride that one.'

The last thing she wanted was this man's company while she rode. She'd had enough of his flirtatious banter and the amusement that never left his sensual mouth even when he wasn't smiling. She'd had enough of the dark eyes that watched her every movement as if he were a mountain cat stalking his next meal, and she'd definitely had enough of the easy sense of intimacy the man had been extending ever since she'd met him.

Even before she'd met him, Ellie thought, frowning as Ben Kolter selected a saddle and slipped it on the roan as if he hadn't heard her answer. His song had been as teasingly seductive as a lover's touch. That was why she hated it so much. The man touched her any time he liked, as if he had every right to satisfy his whims.

'I want to be alone,' she insisted. 'I have some problems to work out.'

'Lighten up, lady. Life isn't half as serious as you pretend it is.' Then he grew more serious himself as he gave her a sidelong glance. 'You shouldn't ride alone at night, anyway. If I were your daddy, I wouldn't let you do it.'

'My daddy . . .' Ellie stopped herself and inhaled a breath to stop her furious response. 'My *father* doesn't tell me what to do, Mr Kolter,' she said evenly. 'No man has ever told me what to do.'

'Maybe it's time one did,' he suggested as he tightened the saddle straps and checked them. He led Lindy Luck to the door of the stables and then he swung up into the saddle with an easy grace that Ellie didn't miss. 'Let's ride off your nasty mood,' he challenged as he turned the horse around to wait for her. 'Then we can get down to the real reason you lured me out here to the stables.'

Was the man serious? she wondered, staring at his handsome face. Or was that his crude idea of a joke? Either way, it didn't matter. The man had an ego the size of Montana and the sensitivity of a rock. Ellie led Sir Reginald through the stable door and swung up into the saddle, turning only slightly to give the man a dismissing smile. 'Goodnight, Mr Kolter. It was nice seeing you for the last time.'

She was irritated by the man's presumption when he followed her along the trail behind the stables. Maybe he thought she was playing a flirtatious game, pretending to say no when yes was what she really meant to say. Or maybe he'd been serious when he said she shouldn't ride alone at night.

That was presumptuous, too. She was a good horsewoman and she knew these trails as well as she knew the palm of her own hand. She wasn't a frail little flower of femininity like Sara-Jean. Maybe it was time she proved that to him. She urged her gelding forward, gaining speed as she crossed the meadow and headed for the pathway through the woods.

The moon floated like a huge white galleon in the sky, and the ground was coated by a silvery light that transformed the earth into the landscape of a dream. Sir Reginald's hoofbeats struck a rhythmic cadence against the frost-hardened ground, but no matter how fast she urged him on or how suddenly she turned to follow a divergent pathway, the sound of another set of hoofbeats kept ringing in her ears.

Ben Kolter followed with a relentless ease. He followed her across the open meadows where the vault of sky arched up like a canopy of velvet sewn with the cold glitter of a billion stars, and he followed her through aspen groves where shadows tangled with the moonlight like lovers' arms interwoven in a passionate caress. But he didn't catch her. He didn't even try.

He stayed behind her, just close enough for her to hear the hoofbeats of his horse. When she slowed, he slowed too, maintaining an even distance that worked on her tired nerves.

Why didn't he catch up? she wondered, reining in Sir Reginald and turning him around to face the aspen grove behind her. That was what she wanted now. She had run off her fury in an exuberant dash across the countryside with the cold night air flowing like water across her wind-whipped cheeks. And now that her fury had dissolved into the physical exhilaration of her flight, she wanted him beside her, taking her into his arms with a firm command she couldn't fight. She wanted to feel his mouth against her throat, insistent and seductive as he laid her back against the ground and took her will away with a touch like fire against her willing flesh. She wanted . . .

. . . To regain her senses. Ellie shook her head impatiently to push the idle dream away. She'd have to be certifiably insane to let this egotistical no-talent cowboy into her bed. What she had was an inconvenient case of lust for the least attractive man on earth. But just because she had an itch, that didn't mean she had to scratch it. She had more brains than that.

Even so, it was difficult to control her wary sense of excitement as Ben Kolter crested the small rise and reined in his horse ten feet away. They sat there for a moment, each taking the measure of the other in a gaze that told too much. Ellie was filled with a mindless panic as Ben brought Lindy Luck out of the shadows and into the moon-drenched clarity of the mountain clearing. 'Do you know what I think about when I see you on television?' he broke their silence finally.

'Everybody in Boulder knows what you think about.'

'I wonder what you do with your hair at night.' He ignored her sarcastic comment. 'Do you brush it down across your shoulders? Or do you braid it into a funny little pigtail that swings across your back every time you take a step?'

'I take it off and put it in my dresser drawer.' She forced her voice to an even, bantering tone as she gave him an answer. He had coaxed Lindy Luck even closer now, and she could feel the brush of his leg against hers for just a moment before Sir Reginald gave a nervous whinny and took a dancing sidestep along the frozen trail.

'I think you wear it in a braid.' His voice had fallen into a low, hoarse murmur, but there was conviction in his tone. And he was right. That unnerved her most of all. The man had a way of guessing the most intimate details of her life, and she was helpless to outstep him in this wary minuet they danced.

'I'll bet it's pretty.' Again his leg brushed hers and this time, before she could stop him, he reached up and removed her hat, exposing her blonde hair to the sheen of silver moonlight. 'Why do you hide it?' His voice was as appreciative as the eyes that studied her flushed face.

'It's cold out here. Only a fool would ride without a hat.'

'I don't mean now,' he disagreed, holding her hat in his gloved hand as he slid down from his horse. 'I mean the rest of the time—on television. You wear that beautiful hair all wrapped up in a prison at the back of your neck. And you hide that gorgeous body of yours in something a lady lawyer would wear to a negotiating session. You should show off your best assets, not disguise them.'

'My *mind* is my best asset, Mr Kolter,' she responded coolly, irritated that he was so much like every other man. She had a degree in journalism and a minor in music history. Why, then did every article about her always start with a description of her looks?

'Not from where I stand.' His voice was teasingly amused. 'Do you want your hat back, Ellie?'

'Yes.'

'Then bring your delicious body down here and get it,' he challenged, reaching up to catch Sir Reginald's bridle and slip it from her hand. 'You can leave your mind up there.'

'You're a Neanderthal!' Ellie seethed as she slipped down from her horse's back. 'You are the most insulting man I've ever . . .' She got no further with her words before Ben caught her up and stopped her with a kiss.

She pulled her mouth away from his and braced her palms against his heavy sheepskin jacket. 'I don't suppose you've ever heard of asking?' she snapped furiously, but Ben was undeterred by her sullen anger. His arms tightened around her just enough to trap her against the strength of his lean chest.

'May I kiss you, Eleanora?' he asked with such formality that the words were doubly derisive.

'No!'

'That takes care of asking,' he responded as he seized her wrists and pulled them back behind her. 'Don't pretend to be outraged,' he warned when she stiffened in his arms. 'You knew I was going to kiss you the minute I saddled that horse. If you didn't want me to, you would have run back to your daddy's house and locked the door behind you.'

She *had* known it would come to this. He could read that much honesty in her restlessly evasive eyes, but Ellie was infuriated by his cocky self-assurance. 'I wanted to go riding,' she insisted. 'On *my* land, with *my* horse.'

'With *your* man following behind you,' he suggested evenly as his fingers touched and lingered on the velvet lapel of her riding jacket. 'Be honest with yourself, Ellie. You may dislike me, but you feel the excitement between us just as much as I do.'

And if she was honest with herself . . . what then? Ellie wondered, confused by the longing that rose so forcefully inside her. She wanted this man, but it was a desire that was as primitive as lust alone. It would be a transient encounter to satisfy a physical attraction. Maybe that was enough to satisfy the cowboy, but her standards were a little higher.

You're the last person who should be talking about honesty.'

'I've been following you for an hour, lady,' he continued in a voice so hoarse and filled with hunger that Ellie felt a shiver of anticipation flow across her trembling senses as he coaxed her closer still. 'Can I be any more honest than that?'

'I think it would be best . . .' Why were her words so stiff and stilted, like ice being forced past her tightened throat? . . . 'if we didn't act on our baser impulses,' she managed to blurt out, wincing at the quicksilver grin that edged upward at the corners of Ben Kolter's mouth. Even her honesty amused him.

'I think it would be best if you stopped talking, Eleanora,' he suggested firmly. His hand cradled the base of her head so completely that she couldn't step away. She was his to kiss. His to command, she understood as his mouth fell against her lips again. She steeled herself against the passion in that touch but she had already tested her will against the greater strength of his and found herself unequal to the match.

Ellie closed her eyes and felt herself swept up in an emotion that hurtled her beyond the boundaries of her senses, past common sense and fear to a realm where all that mattered was the easy movement of his mouth on hers. He demanded her response and, despite her stubbornness, she gave it, lifting her mouth to his in sacrifice to his demanded entry.

His fingers bit into her shoulder blades, but she didn't notice that, so caught up was she in the flood of her own unleashed desires. Then, just as desire had flowed like a rising sea between them, it ebbed back again. 'Well . . .' he whispered appreciatively as his mouth softened and then slid away from hers. 'You're not entirely an iceberg, are you, Eleanora?'

'No . . .' She sucked in a breath of sharp, cold air as his mouth traced a course across her cheek and lingered on her hair. His arms had softened their hold around her, and with the loosening of their bonds a wariness returned to Ellie's mind. The man was a total stranger despite the primitive emotions that flowed across her when he touched her.

'Your ear is cold,' he whispered as he nuzzled his nose against it. 'Do you want your hat?'

'Yes.'

Ben reluctantly released his hold. 'Are you all right?' he asked, studying her face as she took the hat from his extended hand and pulled it across her hair. 'That kiss was a little more than I expected.'

'I'm fine.' She didn't have to fake the breathless uncertainty that trembled in her voice. Even though he had let her go, the passion that had united them still lingered like an echo in her mind. Her mouth still felt the fierceness of his possession, and her legs trembled underneath her as she met his coal-dark eyes. The hunger in his eyes was softened by concern now, and she found that emotion far more troubling than any promise of a renewed passion.

'I'm fine,' she repeated far more firmly, stepping restlessly away before he could take her in his arms again and control her senses. 'Could I have a cigarette?' she asked. 'You have one, don't you?'

'Sure.' He pulled out a pack and handed one to her, then cupped his hand around the lighter to shield the flame as it shivered in the wind. He watched her as she exhaled a sighing breath of smoke that twisted in the air between them. 'I came here tonight to apologise,' he admitted slowly. 'I shouldn't have goaded you during that interview. I thought I was doing you a favour by letting people see the tough and feisty woman I saw in you, but I didn't have any right to make a decision like that for you. I'd like you to forgive me, Ellie.'

She wanted to forgive him, she realised as his hand fell softly to her shoulder in a pleading touch. She wanted far more from this man than she had ever wanted from any man before. 'I'd like us to stop hurting each other,' he continued in a soft, regretful voice. 'Let's leave the past behind and declare a truce. Now. Before either one of us lashes out again.'

'Oh.' Ellie was filled with a sudden nauseated understanding. He wanted to declare a truce before she slapped an injunction on his song. That was all that mattered to him—his own success. For one delirious moment in his arms she had thought that he was offering her a desire that sprang from deep inside him. But this was merely business. It was sugar-coated and seductive, but it was business nonetheless. 'You made a fool of me in that interview,' she reminded him.

'You didn't look like a fool, Ellie,' he said with calculated earnestness. 'But I'm sorry if you feel that way. Tell me how to make it up to you, and I will.'

How could he make it up to her? she wondered bitterly. He had hurt her again by pretending to a passion that he didn't really feel. And he would go on hurting her if she let herself trust the seductive man. His passion was no more real than what Sara-Jean pretended to feel for Ernest Martin. They were two of a kind—two conniving people who weren't above using others for their own gain.

They were two of a kind, Ellie thought, seeing a possible solution to one mess at least. 'There *is* something you could do for me,' she said, dropping her half-smoked cigarette and watching as it went out on the frost-covered ground.

'Anything, Ellie.'

Sara-Jean was a young woman with a young woman's appetites. And Ben Kolter was certainly an attractive man, if one could get past the crassness of his music and the barrier of his monumental ego. What would happen if Sara-Jean had to make a choice between a young man and an old one? Even with all his money, Ernest Martin couldn't compete with Ben Kolter's blatantly suggestive charm.

'I'd like you to see Sara-Jean.'

Ben withdrew his hand from her shoulder, and there was a long moment of silence before he answered. 'See her?' he repeated warily. 'Or sleep with her?'

'Sleep with her,' Ellie matched his bluntness. 'You wouldn't find that too unpleasant, would you?'

'No.' He took out a cigarette and lit it, exhaling an impatient breath of air. 'What makes you think she'd sleep with *me*?'

Because I would have, Ellie thought with an

honesty she didn't care to feel. In the moment when he had taken possession of her mouth and then her trembling senses, she would have done whatever the man asked. Sara-Jean would feel no less for the man who had been her idol since she was a teenager. 'Sara-Jean's simple-minded enough to believe in flattery,' she answered with complete assurance. 'All you have to do is repeat the same act you just tried on me and she'll give you anything you want. I'm willing to pay you for your time.'

'How much?'

'Five thousand dollars,' she responded, disappointed that he was considering the deal.

'Five thousand dollars?' His answer was a laugh, sharp and coldly derisive in the air behind her. 'Gosh, Miss Ellie, five thousand U.S. of A. dollars just for doing what a cowboy does naturally? Golly gee!'

'You want more?'

'I'll make twice that in one night when I get to the top.'

'But you need *Eleanora* to get to the top,' Ellie reminded him. 'I'll tell my lawyer to withdraw my request for an injunction,' she blurted out before she had a chance to think. 'That's what you've been after all night, isn't it? Stop Sara-Jean from marrying my father, and you can keep your grubby little song on the market,' she offered, unnerved by the man's stiff-shouldered posture and the grim eyes that no longer met her stare.

'Stop the injunction first,' he countered, dropping the cigarette to the ground and crushing it with his heel. 'Then I'll see what I can do about Sara-Jean.'

'How do I know that you'll go through with your end of the bargain?'

'You don't,' Ben snapped unpleasantly. 'But I'd be a fool to trust you now that I know what you're willing to do to your own father.'

'You don't know the first thing about my father.'

No. But I know more than I care to know about you,' he answered, stepping forward suddenly to seize her arm. 'You don't know what it feels like to be in love, do you?' His voice had lowered to a resonating whisper. 'Do you know what it feels like to have the whole world light up when someone walks into the room, and to have it go dim again when that person walks away?'

He did, Ellie understood instinctively as his hand cupped her trembling chin and lifted it roughly so he could meet her eyes. For one long moment she wondered what it would be like to love a man that completely. And to be loved that completely in return. 'Do you know?' he demanded brusquely.

'No,' Ellie answered in a shaky voice. She had never had the time to fall in love.

Ben's mouth moved outward into a cold, malicious smile. 'Sara-Jean does. She glows whenever your father touches her. I'll bet she lights up like a Fourth of July carnival when he makes love to her. She's probably the most incredible woman the old man has ever had.

Especially if your momma was anything like you.'

'Will you stop this?' Ellie tried to pull her head away, but Ben's hand tightened to hold it still.

'No. I'm not going to stop,' he answered evenly. 'I'm going to tell you the truth about yourself and Sara-Jean. You're so damn jealous of her that you can't see straight. She doesn't have your brains, or your looks, or your clothes, or your fancy little car, but when she walks into the room your father doesn't even know that you're alive. That's what bothers you, isn't it? You're not afraid he's being taken for a ride. You wish he were.'

'Sara-Jean is after his . . . '

'Shut up!' Ben demanded curtly. 'I'm not finished yet.'

Ellie pressed her lips together. 'That's better,' Ben murmured as his thumb edged up to trace the stubborn outline of her mouth. 'Take my advice and forget about her,' he suggested. 'Come to my bed, Ellie. Let me make love to you, and maybe you'll stop worrying about all the Sara-Jaens in this world who have something you don't have.'

Ellie pulled away from his arms before she succumbed to the insistent invitation in his eyes. 'You're not my type, Mr Kolter.'

'I'm not good enough for you?' he asked. 'But I'm good enough for Sara-Jean, aren't I?' he guessed in a voice that was mockingly unpleasant. 'We're two hicks from the hill country. Is that what you're thinking?' She didn't answer.

'You're a beaut, lady,' Ben said derisively. 'You're a class A snob with ice-water in your veins. Would you like to hear something amusing?' he demanded as he stopped beside his roan and smoothed his hand along the horse's neck. 'I was going to ask the Nashville people to refilm the interview because it bothered you so much. And the act you accused me of performing . . . Well,' he smiled unpleasantly, 'maybe some day you'll figure it out, Eleanora. File for an injunction,' he challenged as he swung up into his saddle. 'You'll need it when I get done with you.'

With that last remark, he turned the horse around and disappeared into the darkness of the trees. Ellie listened to the hoofbeats until the last echo disappeared and only the sound of her own heartbeat thundered in her ears.

CHAPTER FIVE

IT WAS over. Sara-Jean was Mrs Ernest Martin

Ellie parked her car in the car park of the Diablo Club and stared up numbly at the flickering red neon devil that danced a hypnotic two-step above the door of the restaurant and bar. She had received a telegram that afternoon.

'Eloped. Will be at Dulac Hotel, St Martin until January 15. Father.'

No 'Hope you understand'. No 'Sorry you couldn't be here'. Nothing beyond the hard, cold facts. At least Sara-Jean had been more gracious. A letter had arrived in the afternoon mail, telling Ellie that by the time she had received it Sara-Jean and Ernest Martin would be married.

'I love your father very much,' she had written in a graceful, looping hand. 'I hope I can be the kind of wife he needs. That doesn't mean I'm going to push you out of the house or out of your father's life. He loves you, Ellie, even though he doesn't say it very well. I hope we can be friends some day. Sara-Jean.'

It was over, Ellie thought morosely. Sara-Jean was Mrs Ernest Martin. Now there would be children. A son, she thought with a twist of jealousy she didn't want to feel. Ernest Martin would finally have the child he'd always wanted.

There was no use crying over it or feeling bitter for her father's blindness to how she felt. His selfishness might hurt, but she didn't have the power to change him any more than she could change the nature of the granite mountains or the rising of the sun. Any more than she could change Ben Kolter, Ellie thought as her eyes drifted to the sign beside the Diablo Club's main door.

The Travelling Asylum Band, it read in large black letters. Below that there was a photograph she couldn't quite make out, but she knew that he was there, handsome and self-assured, laughing at her as he gazed out from the picture.

In the past three weeks he'd done everything he could to show his contempt for Eleanora Martin. He'd given half a dozen interviews on the radio and in the local papers, repeating his theory that the Boulder iceberg could be melted by a man like him. 'But a man would have to kidnap her to get the chance,' he always ended with a laugh. 'And I don't have time for that kind of charity.'

'The man lacks more than time,' Ellie had snapped an unfortunate answer to a reporter. The comment had been printed in the papers beneath a picture of Ben Kolter.

The Nashville programme had aired, followed by an annoucement that the Travelling Asylum Band was planning to do a video of *Eleanora*. And the song was moving relentlessly up the country music charts. It now was number six. She couldn't go anywhere without people asking about Ben Kolter.

'You look like six kinds of hell these days,' her

producer had commented the night before. 'Is it this Kolter business?'

'No. I have a touch of the 'flu, that's all.'

Even Ernest Martin was concerned. 'I misjudged the man,' he had grunted over the morning paper a few days before. 'Well, never mind. I'll find a way to stop him.'

Stopping Ben Kolter was only half of it, Ellie understood. She had to stop the insane longing that had seized her ever since the man had walked into her life. He was there even in her dreams, reaching out to touch her with a hand so warm and promising she moaned with a desire to be in his arms and turned against her pillow until she woke into an empty loneliness that grew colder with each night.

Their public feuding had to stop. That was why she was here, she told herself as she stepped out of her car and made her way to the club door. But even as she thought that, she knew she was lying to herself. She wanted to see him again. It didn't matter that he hated her or that his vendetta had come close to shattering her nerves. She was obsessed by the handsome country singer, like every other groupie who followed him from club to club, weaving every glance into a fantasy that encompassed the two of them alone.

'Stay away from all the desperadoes who would sing a song like this one in your ear . . .' Ben's voice was the first thing she noticed as she stepped into the darkened, smoke-filled room. 'Stay away from men who tell you one thing, then do another when you're near . . .'

Ellie made her way round the edge of the

crowded room and found a table at the back, easing herself down into the anonymity of the shadows. The room was mercifully dark, and everyone was watching the performance. If she was lucky, no one would notice her.

'What can I get you, honey?' It was the waitress who had stopped beside her table, and the woman grinned when she recognised Ellie's face. 'I'll be . . . It's Eleanora Martin! Hey, Frank, Eleanora Martin's going to review the place tonight,' she called to the man behind the bar.

Oh, lord, Ellie thought, wincing as people turned to stare at her far too recognisable face. Now the ridicule would start.

'Hey, Kolter!' A drunken call went up. 'Your girlfriend's here!'

'Is that right?' Ben's voice drifted back on a haze of smoke and laughter. 'Which one?'

'Eleanora.'

'So, what can I get you to drink?' the waitress prompted as Ellie stared numbly ahead, trying to control her anger and her pain. He would sing *Eleanora* now, giving it a sarcastic, cutting edge that would ridicule her even more.

'I don't know . . . Anything . . .'

'Bring her what Kolter drinks,' a man at the next table suggested.

He hated her, but it hadn't always been that way. There had been moments when the craggy remoteness of his face had softened and he had shown her a sympathetic kindness. But she had ruined that small glimmer of friendship and alliance by asking him to seduce Sara-Jean. She'd been

wrong to do that. That was what she had come
to tell him, but now she'd lost the courage.

'Shall I bring you another one when this is
finished?'

Ellie looked up, startled, as the waitress placed
a drink in front of her. Only then did she realise
that Ben was singing *Eleanora*. 'Yes. Thank you.'
She curled her hand around it and lifted it to take
a sip.

Ellie watched as Ben picked up a glass from the
floor in front of him and downed half of it in one
thirsty swallow. He'd had six drinks to her three
and she was feeling the effects. The noise inside
the crowded club was amplified until it throbbed
against her like an unwelcome touch, and Ben
Kolter's music seemed to play inside her head like
a taunting echo of her own regrets.

'One last song before we call it quits,' Ben's
voice announced in a voice as smooth as satin.
'How about a love song to put you all in the
mood for taking your pretty ladies home?'

Ben's fingers played across the strings, then he
lifted his voice to sing. 'There are thousands of
birds up above me . . . And millions of fish in the
sea . . . There are flowers galore, then quite a bit
more . . . But only one woman for me . . .' His
lilting voice reached her like a touch and smoothed
across her weary senses, inviting her to join the
teasing humour of his song.

She'd been wrong to try to hurt him. He had
offered her a moment of desire and she had been
too frightened to trust the honesty of that. But

now she understood it and longed for another chance to set things right between them.

Would Ben understand how frightened and alone she had felt that night? Would he understand how difficult it was to chart a course between the disppointments of the past and the unknown pleasures of the future? Maybe he would. There had been moments when she had looked into his eyes and read a sympathetic understanding of life's pain.

'There are billions of stars in the heavens . . . They stretch to infinity . . . Grains of sand at the shore, and then Eleanore . . .' Ben let the word string out to get a laugh before he finished with a flourish against the strings. 'There's only one woman for me . . .'

It was a laugh at her expense, she knew, feeling her heart tighten inside her chest. He wouldn't understand her regrets or her faltering apologies even if she could find the courage to explain them to the man. If she stayed and tried to tell him, he would only laugh at her again. She gathered up her coat and bag and slipped out of the door before he had a chance to leave the stage.

She had no courage at all where Ben Kolter was concerned. Not an ounce of it, she thought as she fumbled through her bag, searching for her keys.

'Do me a favour . . .' The voice behind her was cool and even. Ben's voice, Ellie knew, trying to compose her face into an even mask before she turned around. 'Leave the rest of the band out of it this time.'

'What?'

'When you do your review, don't cut the rest of
them to shreds just because you're furious at me.
If it makes a difference to you, Murphy has
nominated me for Bastard of the Year, based on
my performance the past few weeks.'

He thought she had come to do another review
of the Travelling Asylum Band. Now was the time
for courage, Ellie knew. 'I didn't come to do a
review,' she admitted in a whisper. 'I came to tell
you that I'm sorry.'

Ben didn't answer, but his eyes registered
surprise and a wary curiosity. 'I'm apologising,'
she admitted, opening her bag again and searching
for her keys. Even when she found them, they
seemed strange and heavy in her hand.

'Are you drunk?' Ben asked suspiciously.

'A little.' She gave him a sheepishly embarrassed
smile. Now that she was outside in the cold air
her head was whirling dizzily. 'Why? Do you
think it's dangerous to apologise when I've been
drinking?'

'Apologise all you want. Just don't drive,' he
answered tersely, taking the keys from her gloved
hand and unlocking her car door. 'Get in and
slide over,' he commanded. 'I don't want you to
wrap yourself around a tree on my account.'

That was an interesting statement coming from
the man who had driven her half crazy in the past
few weeks. Even her father had asked her what
she could have done to make Ben Kolter hate her
so completely.

'It wouldn't do you any harm,' she murmured
as he turned the key in the ignition and backed
the car out into the road. 'You could come to my

funeral and place a single . . . What?' She closed
her eyes to think. 'Not a rose. That's too common.
A man like you would think of something just a
little different. Daisies,' she remembered what
he'd said about her name, 'you could place a
single white daisy on my grave. I can see the
picture in *People* magazine now. "Ben Kolter
mourns for Eleanora." It would sell a million
records.'

The cowboy didn't answer, but neither did he
look amused.

Ellie leaned back against the seat and stared
wistfully out of the window at the Christmas
decorations that had transformed ordinary little
bungalows into gingerbread houses decorated with
glowing candy confections. She had always been
jealous of the children who lived in houses like
those. She imagined them gathered around the
fireplace on Christmas Eve, popping corn and
stringing cranberries and singing Christmas carols
with parents who adored them. With parents who
adored each other, Ellie admitted to herself. The
way her father adored Sara-Jean.

'They eloped this morning.'

'I see.'

Ben didn't say any more than that, and Ellie
leaned her head against the seat, feeling her
loneliness close in more tightly with every mile
that drew her closer to her home. He'd leave her
at the door, then he'd go away. Well, whose fault
was that but her own? she asked herself impatiently.
She certainly hadn't offered him anything to make
him stay.

Ellie sighed as he stopped her Lamborghini in

front of her father's empty house. He had wanted
her once. And she had wanted him. She had been
obsessed by a physical desire for this man ever
since she'd met him. Maybe she should sleep with
him and get him out of her system so she could
get on with her life again.

But even as she thought that, she knew it
wouldn't be that way. She wasn't the type to love
a man one night and pretend it didn't matter
when he left her in the morning. And Kolter was
the type to leave.

'Is this the house key?' Ben asked as he opened
up her door and held out a hand to help her from
the car.

'Yes.' She made a concerted effort to steady
her legs underneath her as she followed him up
the walkway to the house. Now he would leave,
she knew. And that was the last thing in the
world she wanted.

'I'll call a cab to get back to the club,' he
confirmed her fears.

She wanted him to hold her in his arms. She
remembered the strength she had felt there when
she had slipped down from her horse and been
caught up in his embrace. And she remembered,
too, the pleasure she had felt when his insistent
mouth had carried her beyond the boundaries of
thought to a realm where she existed only as a
woman under his appreciative caress.

'It's true what they say about you,' she
commented as he slid the key into the door and
gave it a sharp turn. 'You can hold your alcohol
better than any man I've ever met. You had twice
as many drinks as I did.'

'I wasn't counting,' he said tersely as he opened up the door.

'Is everything else true, too?' Ellie slid her coat away from her shoulders and left it on a chair as she followed him into the study. He was supposed to be as good at handling women as he was at handling alcohol. And every bit as eager to prove that it was true. 'What they say about you and women?' she prompted as he leaned across her father's desk and found the Boulder phonebook. 'Are all those stories true?'

'I was drinking iced tea,' he admitted wearily. 'It's all part of the hype, lady.'

And so were the stories about the women, Ellie guessed. And everything he'd said about wanting her. The only thing that ruled him was ambition, but at this moment she was too drunk to care.

'Would you like to stay?' she asked with drunken bluntness. 'You find me attractive, don't you? With my cool green eyes the colour of the Arctic sea . . .' She took the words from his own taunting song. 'I know we haven't always got along, but I still . . .' She faltered under the cold surprise of his stare. 'Well?' she asked impatiently. 'Do you find me attractive?'

'You're not a bad-looking woman,' he answered carefully.

'Would you like to stay?'

'Are you asking me to make love to you?'

'Yes.' Her answer was a whisper, and she turned away before she met the mockery in his eyes. Why did she always end up making a fool of herself with this man? Ellie wondered desperately. Why did every conversation end with her humiliation? 'You don't think much of me, do you?' she found the courage to ask.

'I think you're a brat,' he admitted honestly. 'A snob, and right now a tipsy one. Do you want me to elaborate on any of those points?'

'No,' she answered in a whisper, staring out of the window to the driveway where he had parked her car. Why did it matter what he thought of her?

'Well, I will anyway,' he offered coldly. 'Your apology fooled me for a minute, but I know what kind of game you're playing now, and I'd have to be a fool to go along with it. I make love to you tonight, and in the morning you call your father to tell him that Ben Kolter took advantage of your drunken misery. That should bring him back here in a hurry. All your life he's given you everything you've ever wanted. But you can't even let him spend his honeymoon in peace.'

'You're wrong,' Ellie said defensively. 'My father has never given me anything I wanted.'

'I suppose you found the Lamborghini under a cabbage leaf?'

'Do you think I care about that car?' Her patience snapped at last. Maybe she had misjudged Ben Kolter, but he had misjudged her, too. 'Or about designer clothes or expensive jewellery?' she asked, finding a bottle of Scotch on the sideboard bar and pouring herself a drink to calm her trembling nerves. 'Do you honestly think money matters to me, Mr Kolter? Do you remember that story about the obstetrician that you found so amusing? Well, I've heard that story all of my life. The first thing I did on earth was disppoint my father because I wasn't the son he wanted. And I went right on disappointing him, no matter how hard I tried. All the time I was at boarding school I used to dream that he would call me and say, "I want you to come home." And he finally did. I had a job in Boston, but he said he needed me, so I came home without a question.

'He needed me because my mother was dying.' she explained. 'And he didn't have the time to pay attention to her. I'm the one who sat with her and read to her. And in the end I was the one who dressed her and bathed her and gave her her medication because my wonderful father who has given me everything was too busy to come home from the office. He wasn't even here the night she died. But *now* he has the time for Sara-Jean. Isn't that wonderful?' she asked sarcastically. '*Now* he can take time off from work. *Now* he's going to the Caribbean for a month-long honeymoon because he's finally discovered that love is all that matters in this life. Now he wants a child. I wonder what the hell he thinks I am,' she said bitterly. 'All I want is for my father to say something . . . I'm sorry would be enough, or I love . . . Damn,' she muttered hoarsely as the hot tears welled up in her eyes and coursed across her cheeks. 'I don't know why I still care about him. Or you, either . . .' She wiped her tears away with her cool palm and took a breath to stop her snaking sobs. 'You're as selfish as he is.'

Ben didn't answer, and Ellie didn't turn around to see if there was any expression on his sternly handsome face. Why did it matter what the cowboy thought of her? He had never liked her and he never would. 'I've been sending out resumés and tapes,' she admitted in a firmer voice. 'As soon as I can get another job, I'll get out of my father's life so he can start all over again with a brand new baby. Maybe he'll do a better job this time.'

Ben didn't say a word, but when she lifted her glass to take a sip, he reached out to take it from her hand. 'You've had enough to drink, Ellie,' he cautioned in a voice that held no derision now. 'You're not going to solve anything this way.'

'I know,' she admitted honestly, so tired now that she could barely think. She wouldn't solve anything by sleeping with Ben Kolter, either, although she longed to lose herself in the warmth of the strong arms that folded around her so protectively.

'I shouldn't have offered you money to make love to Sara-Jean,' she admitted, pressing her face against his shoulder as the tears flowed down her cheeks again. 'No wonder you hate me.'

'Hush, Ellie,' Ben said softly, touching her hair with an unexpectedly gentle hand. 'I haven't been a saint, either.'

'I was afraid of being hurt . . . but I didn't mean . . .' Her words escaped between the convulsive sobs that shook her slender shoulders, and Ben tightened his hold around her as if he were her lifeline to a calmer shore. '. . . to hurt . . .'

'Ssh,' he insisted, pressing his mouth against her yellow hair. 'I'm going to cry, too, if you don't stop,' he pleaded. But now that she had found her courage, there was no way to stop her misery from pouring out.

'I'm everything you said I am. A snob and a spoiled brat . . . I wanted to apologise,' she moaned as his arm tightened to pull her closer to his chest. 'But I lost my courage, so I had a drink. And then I had another and another . . .'

'I know the syndrome,' he said wryly, keeping one arm around her as he searched through his pocket for a cotton handkerchief. 'Here. Blow your nose and we'll start again.'

'Thank you.' Ellie pressed her lips together to stop a renewed wave of sobs as she wiped her tears away. 'I know I'm an iceberg . . .'

'You're not that cold.'

The room was whirling dizzily and Ellie reached out unconsciously for the reassuring comfort of Ben's shoulder as she stumbled clumsily against him. He caught her up just as her knees buckled underneath her. Then he lifted her against his chest and carried her up the stairs to the second floor. 'Where's your bedroom?'

'Down the hall,' answered Ellie, letting her head fall against his shoulder where it seemed that nature had carved a perfect place for it to lie. 'This one . . .'

Ben used his hip to open up the door, then laid her on the blue chintz coverlet of her bed. 'Ohh . . .' Ellie groaned as she closed her eyes. The room was swaying like a ship caught in a storm and there was a disconcerting knot at the pit of her stomach. 'I don't like being drunk,' she admitted, wincing as he pulled her up to a sitting position. 'I've been stupid.'

'You're entitled,' Ben said tersely as he unbuttoned her dress and pushed it off her shoulders. 'It's part of being human.'

'It sounds like a Ben Kolter song . . .' Her head lolled forward until it struck his shoulder. 'I was drunk and human. Do-wah diddy . . . Hm,' she murmured as his hand swept up her back.

He smelled so good, Ellie thought as her face fell against his throat and she inhaled the musky sweet aroma of his aftershave. And she felt so right here in his arms.

'You're going to have a hangover the size of Siberia in the morning,' predicted Ben as he pulled her slip over her head and tossed it on the floor. He coaxed her back against the pillows and removed the rest of the her clothes before he pulled the blankets up around her. Then he stretched himself beside her and coaxed her face against his shoulder. 'I'll stay until you fall asleep,' he offered, laying a soft hand against her hair. 'You can trust me not to hurt you, Ellie.'

She did trust him, Ellie realised, letting her heavy eyelids close. It made no sense at all, but she knew the cowboy wouldn't hurt her.

CHAPTER SIX

ELLIE stared at the boxes of glittery ornaments that she'd taken down from the attic, but no matter how hard she tried she couldn't raise any enthusiasm for the task of decorating the large balsam tree that stood in the corner of the room.

She eased herself down to the couch instead and sipped the eggnog she had made, surprised by how flat and lifeless it could taste. She had put her favourite record on the stereo, but even that was giving her little pleasure now. She longed for something far more lively, and the tune that leaped to mind was the refrain of *Eleanora*. She longed for Ben, she admitted to herself, wondering why she should think of only him tonight. There were half a dozen Christmas Eve parties she could have gone to. But Ben wouldn't have been invited to any of them.

The man didn't even like her, she reminded herself, although she couldn't help remembering the strong arms that had folded around her just a few days before. He had carried her up the winding stairway to her bedroom and had laid her gently on her bed. Then he had stayed. Ellie didn't know how long, but when she had awakened in the morning, there had been a percolator of strong, black coffee waiting on her dresser.

'Nothing happened, Ellie.' She had read the scrawled words on the note she'd found propped against a coffee cup. 'I stayed to make sure you'd be all right.'

She had been vulnerable and helpless and he hadn't hurt her. But he hadn't called her, either. It had been four days and she hadn't heard from him at all.

The doorbell rang so unexpecedly that Ellie almost spilled her eggnog. 'Who is it?' she called out, trying to still the hope that rose too painfully inside her.

'Santa Claus.' It was Ben's voice, and Ellie could imagine the smile that must be quirking outward on his face. 'I can't find your chimney.'

'It's on the roof.'

'Ah.' His eyes sparkled as she unlocked the door and pulled it open. 'I didn't look there. Hi,' he smiled as his eyes flickered downward, taking in her red silk dress. 'You're going out tonight, aren't you?'

'No . . . Not right away.' Why was she so happy to see him? Ellie wondered, stepping back to gesture him inside. 'I've been invited to a couple of Christmas Eve parties, but I . . .' Don't want to go, she realised as she meet his curious brown eyes. She wanted to be here with him, her head resting in that triangle of space his shoulder formed when he held her close. 'Would you like to come in and have a cup of eggnog?' she changed the subject nervously. 'I make a very good eggnog.'

'I imagine you do.' Ben glanced around the

room, noting the bare tree and the stack of boxes. 'Is there anything you don't do well?'

'Sometimes I don't drink wisely,' she admitted, ladling the frothy eggnog into a cup. 'Thank you for driving me home and . . .' She stopped, painfully aware of what he must be thinking. He had undressed her. She could still feel his warm hands smoothing up her thighs to strip off her stockings. ' . . . and for making me the coffee,' she ended feebly, handing him the cup. 'I called the ranch to thank you, but nobody answered.'

'We were doing a gig in Denver.'

'Oh.' Then he hadn't been avoiding her. 'I suppose we should have a toast.'

'I suppose we should.' Ben lifted his glass in her direction. 'To Christmas,' he proposed. 'When lions lie down with lambs, and cowboys make peace with ladies.'

'Yes.' She was pleased by the offer of a truce. 'To cowboys and to ladies.' Ben's eyes still lingered on her pink, flushed face, and Ellie glanced away, as giddy as a schoolgirl in the throes of a first love. 'I could use some help decorating the tree,' she suggested evenly. 'If you do a good job, I might even make you supper.'

'I can't stay.'

'Oh.' He had somewhere else to go. And someone else to be with, Ellie thought, smiling bravely despite the keenness of her disappoinmemnt. 'Well, it's probably just as well,' she said philosophically. 'I'm expected at a party.'

'Will there be kids there?'

'No, I don't think so.'

'That's too bad. Christmas isn't really Christmas without them. Do you like them?' he asked curiously. '*Real* kids,' he elaborated. 'The kind who spill orange juice on your lap and talk about their pet worms during dinner?'

'Yes.' She couldn't help her laugh. 'I like that kind best. Why?'

He smiled, but for once it wasn't a quirky smile of cynical amusement. It was reticent and shy. 'I've got six of them to entertain tonight. They're not mine,' he hastened to explain when her eyebrows rose with an unspoken question. 'They're Murphy's.'

'Six?'

'Yeah.' He sipped his eggnog. 'Four ex-wives. Six kids. The man doesn't learn as fast as I do. Anyhow . . .' He sighed as he turned away and stared at the bare tree. 'I was sent into town for pizzas and I thought maybe I could find someone who likes children enough to help us keep some order at the ranch.'

'Oh . . .'

There was no place she'd rather be tonight, and she knew that he could see that when he turned around to meet her hopeful eyes. 'I was hoping you could help me out,' he suggested evenly. 'Maybe your hosts would understand if you called and told them you have to do a favour for a friend?'

'Yes,' Ellie agreed without a moment's pause for thought, 'I'm sure they would.'

'Nathan, Benjamin, Cleantha.' Ben pointed to the children who were sprawled on the carpeted floor of Murphy's living-room. 'Veronica, better known as Ronnie,' he gestured to a pretty teenager sitting on the couch, 'Jacob, and last but not least, Steven the wonder child.' He leaned down and scooped up a five-year-old, laying him across his shoulder like a giggling sack of grain. 'Steven's the only one of these barbarians who sided with me and voted for a Christmas goose.'

'Steven would side with you if you voted to jump off a bridge,' Ronnie responded with a laugh. Her eyes lingered on Ellie's face, curiously assessing their new guest, then recognition crossed her pretty features. 'Oh, my God. You're Eleanora Martin, aren't you?'

'Ronnie watches a lot of television.' Ben tapped her affectionately on the head. 'Where's your daddy?'

'Out in the barn doing his yearly schtick. So . . .' She glanced suspiciously from Ben to Ellie. 'How come the two of you aren't fighting?'

'Miracles happen on Christmas Eve. Okay, heathen troops, listen up.' Ben set Steven on his feet and raised his hands for silence. 'I've got two announcements to make. First, this pretty lady is Ellie Martin. And . . .' His voice trailed off into a suspense-full whisper. 'The pizzas are in the truck.'

'Geronimo!' Ronnie laughed as five children stampeded for the door. Then she returned her attention to their unexpected guest, noting the shy way that Ellie glanced at Ben for reassurance in the chaotic bedlam of Murphy's family. 'Is this the best date you could get for Christmas Eve?'

'Hey! I'm a class act!' Ben objected, circling Ellie's waist with a protectively warm arm. 'Aren't I, love?'

Yes, he was. But Ellie didn't have a chance to answer his teasing question before the door burst open wide again, letting in a cold burst of wind and the chatter of excited voices.

Ronnie leapt up to collect the pizzas before they were up-ended on the rug. Ellie took some boxes, too, and followed Ronnie to the kitchen. 'What's your father's yearly schtick?' she asked curiously as she laid the pizzas on the table.

'You'll see in a few minutes. When it comes to Christmas, he and Ben are the biggest children in the world.'

Ellie didn't have long to wait. She heard the front door bang open and Murphy's voice boom out. 'Jumpin' criminy! Do you know what just happened in the barn? I was standing there, minding my own business, when the door blew open and in came a flying sleigh!'

'Santa Claus!' A chorus of excited cries met the announcement. Ellie went to the doorway to watch the scene. Murphy looked like Santa Claus himself, with his russet beard and ruddy cheeks and the eyes that twinkled with amusement as he dusted flour from his shoulders.

'I got covered with this magic reindeer dust, and then I had to duck because presents came falling down all around me,' he complained with a pretended peevishness. 'They're still out there, littering the barn floor.'

'Santa's still out there, too,' Ben added as he pulled back the curtain and stared into the night. 'I see something glowing right behind the barn. Can you see it, Ellie?'

'Yes,' she agreed, slipping readily into the spirit of the hoax as she joined Ben at the window. 'Over to the right. I think that glow must be Rudolph's nose.'

'Eleanora Martin?' It was Murphy's turn to be surprised. 'I'll be damned—darned . . .' he corrected quickly, remembering the children. 'He took my advice and did it,' he murmured as a smile spread out across his face. It was all the welcome that Ellie needed, and she smiled back, grateful that she'd been accepted so readily at Sloan Murphy's house.

'I see him!' Steven cried, jostling with his brothers for a space at the window. It was Nathan who proposed they run out to the barn, and once again the door banged open and a draught blew in to ruffle all the papers on the hall table.

'I'd better go along!' Murphy apologised, lifting his hand in a quick greeting before he chased the children to the barn. Ben slipped his arm easily around Ellie's waist in a gesture that pleased her even more because it was so totally unconscious.

'It would be wonderful to be that young again,' she admitted wistfully, watching the children lope across the lawn towards the barn beyond. A single maple tree was hung with coloured lights that glowed against the dark night sky. 'To believe in something . . .'

Ben turned just enough to meet her eyes. 'You don't believe in Santa Claus?' he asked with mock surprise.

'Of course I do,' she matched his teasing tone. 'And I believe in the Easter Bunny and leprechauns and fairies. And . . .' Love, she thought, meeting the warmth in his brown eyes. All kinds of magic seemed possible when she was in his arms. 'Bigfoot and flying saucers . . .' she said instead, noting the way his mouth quirked outward, the left side first, until his lips had parted to show a row of even teeth.

She liked amusing him, she decided, studying his handsome face. Despite his broad smile and glowingly warm eyes, there was a shadowy remoteness there, pockets of old sadness that still lingered like clouds across the sun. Ellie longed to chase those clouds away with the softness of her touch. 'What do *you* believe in?' she asked curiously.

For just a fraction of a moment his eyes darkened and fell before the clear concern in hers. Then his smile was back, teasingly flirtatious and just as solid as a wall that kept her firmly on the other side. 'I believe in pepperoni pizza,' he answered. 'Let's go stake our claim before the thundering herd comes back.'

He coaxed her to the kitchen where Ronnie was setting glasses on a tray. Ellie set to work filling them with ice from a nearby bucket.

'Dad says the band's going on the road as soon as they release their new album.' Ronnie made conversation in a light-hearted tone that was betrayed by the restless darting of her eyes.

'You'll be needing gofers to travel with the band, won't you?'

'I suppose I will,' Ben answered as he took out a stack of napkins and set them on the table. 'Do you know anybody who needs a low-paying job?'

'I could do it,' Ronnie suggested hopefully. 'I could finish my last year of high school by correspondence, and I wouldn't be any trouble. I promise I wouldn't, Ben. And Mom wouldn't mind. She'd be glad to get rid of me.'

Ben didn't answer for a moment. Then he turned back to the kitchen drawer to find the silverware. 'Are you and your mom having a hard time?'

'Yeah. She caught me smoking, and she hit the ceiling.'

'Cigarettes aren't good for you.'

'It wasn't exactly a cigarette.' The confession was delivered in a mumble, then Ronnie shrugged. 'You know how my mom is. She's so uptight about everything, she lectured me for hours. I'm seventeen years old, Ben,' she complained. 'I need to be with people who understand about life. People like you and Dad. Not someone who's going to read me passages from *Readers Digest* every time I smoke a joint.'

'I wouldn't worry about your mother's opinion of drugs,' Ben answered evenly.

'No?' Ronnie's voice was hopeful.

Ellie frowned as she dropped ice cubes into another glass. Ronnie was asking for permission to experiment with drugs, and the adult she adored was giving it!

'No,' Ben repeated grimly. 'If *I* catch you doing drugs, I'll take you apart before your mother gets to you. Hey!' he cried as Ronnie turned away. 'This discussion isn't over.'

'I should have known you wouldn't disagree with . . .' Ronnie stopped when Ben strode up behind her and trapped her in his arms.

'Who's the prettiest girl in the world?' he demanded, tightening his hold when she struggled to break free.

'Oh, Ben. I'm too old for this!'

'Not on Christmas Eve, you're not. Who's the prettiest girl in the world?' he repeated his demand.

'I am,' she admitted with a grimace.

'Who's the smartest girl in the world?'

'I am.'

'Who's going to break a million hearts?'

'I am.' She tried to maintain a bored expression, but a smile twitched upward on her lips. 'Okay, Mr Subtle, I've got the message.'

'Good. Now get your high school diploma, too,' Ben commanded as he let her go. 'But set the dining-room table first.'

'Yes, sir.' Ronnie gathered up the silverware and napkins and disappeared through the kitchen doorway.

'And all this time I thought *I* was the prettiest girl in the world.' Ellie smiled her approval as Ben leaned back against the counter and lit a cigarette.

'Nope.' He let out a long, sighing stream of smoke before he met her eyes with warm appreciation. 'You're the prettiest *woman* in the world. There's a difference, love.'

'Oh.' She couldn't help the flush of pink that suffused her cheeks, and Ben noted it with silent interest. Then he stubbed out his cigarette. 'There's something I've wanted to do for days now, Ellie,' he confessed as he slipped his arms around her waist and coaxed her closer to the warmth of his lean thighs.

'Oh?' She couldn't stop her smile. The cowboy was going to kiss her. 'And what would that be, Mr Kolter?' She met his eyes with a clear invitation and lifted her mouth to his. But his warm lips had barely touched hers when the kitchen door flew open and thudded back against the wall.

'Are the pizzas ready yet?' an excited voice demanded. Ben pulled away from Ellie with a frustrated sigh, and Cleantha gave a childishly delighted giggle.

Ellie sat cross-legged on the couch, inhaling the scents of pine and clove and wood smoke that drifted through the room. The children had been in bed for hours, all except for Ronnie who had decided she was old enough to join the adult conversation. But now even she had drifted sleepily away, leaving Ben and Murphy to talk in the pleasant shorthand way that old friends often talked. Ellie had stopped listening to the content and only heard the reassuring rise and fall of voices.

Her cheek touched Ben's shoulder and she roused herself just enough to pull away, but

Ben's arm circled her to coax her back again. 'I can't keep a woman awake any more,' he joked as Ellie closed her eyes and relaxed trustingly against him.

'We're all getting older,' Murphy agreed good-naturedly as he got up and left the room. A moment later he was back, and Ellie felt the warmth of a down quilt as it was pulled across her. Ben laid her back against the pillows and stretched himself beside her. 'Hm,' she murmured as she pressed her face against his neck and inhaled the musky, rich aroma of his skin. 'You're a very nice man, Ben Kolter. Do you know that?'

'And you're a good sport, Ellie Martin,' he answered, sliding his arm underneath her so he could hold her close. 'A very beautiful good sport.' His fingers touched her hair with an unconscious tenderness and Ellie turned her head enough to see his sad-eyed face, illuminated by the glowing embers on the hearth.

That sadness was always there, etched into his handsome face like scars on a rock cliff that were imperceptible until one took the time to really look. Ellie wondered what Ben Kolter's face had looked like before that weary burden of old pain had settled like a veil across his even features.

'What are you thinking?' she whispered.

'I'm waiting for the shoe to drop,' he confessed with a melancholy smile. 'Tomorrow morning Murphy and I will drive all the kids to the airport to send them back to their mothers, and then Murphy's going to break down and cry. It happens every year.'

'Can we do anything to cheer him up?'

'I'll take him up into the mountains for a few days. We'll get drunk and wallow in self-pity together, then we'll get down to work again.'

On their video, she understood, trying to hide the unhappiness that flickered through her thoughts. The song that had started as a local joke had found its way to the country charts, and he would have to be a fool not to promote it. But it made a fool of her. It was a cruel irony, she thought. The very song that could take Ben Kolter back to the top again might ruin every chance she had to be taken seriously in her profession.

'I need the song, Ellie,' said Ben, as if he could read her mind. 'It doesn't have anything to do with the way I feel about you. It's just business now.'

'You've got other songs. Better ones,' Ellie suggested optimistically. 'You could be successful without exploiting *Eleanora*.'

'I *do* have better songs,' he admitted honestly. 'But none of them are on the country charts. I need to promote *Eleanora* in order to get people to listen to my new album.'

'And if you do promote it, you'll ruin my chances of ever being taken seriously as a television journalist. If business is business, why does it feel so personal?' she asked miserably. 'It's always going to feel personal. No matter how hard we try to separate business from emotion, it's always going to come back to that.'

Ben was silent for a moment, but his face reflected the conflict he was feeling. 'If it were only me, I'd withdraw the song from the market. But you're asking me to take a sure shot at success away from Murphy and Trawler and G.T.'

'I know,' she admitted miserably. Why did love have to be this complicated? If only the world would go away and leave the two of them in peace, maybe they could find a few brief moments of happiness in each other's arms. 'I wish we could find a mountain top somewhere,' she admitted. 'Just for a few hours. We deserve that much.'

'We do,' he agreed, touching her cheek with a regretful sigh. Then he met her eyes as if he were debating what to do. 'The cowboy would very much like to kiss you, lady.'

'The lady would very much like to be kissed,' she admitted honestly. It wouldn't solve a thing, but they deserved some pleasure, no matter how fleeting or how brief.

Ben's mouth met hers softly, with a sweet persuasion that worked a magic no other kind of caress could have done. Ellie clung to his broad shoulders, trusting the pleasure of his mouth as it moved over hers, trusting his gentleness and goodness as he deepened his caress.

In that moment her heart opened to him so completely there seemed no boundaries between them. As he took possession of her mouth, they fell together through a tangled weave of physical desires that electrified her with the immediacy of passion.

It was the worst time and the worst place to lose herself in Ben Kolter's arms. The house was filled with children who could wake at any moment. But Ellie had slipped too far beyond restraint to call herself back from the distant, exotic shore of tumultuous sensation.

It was Ben who brought them back. He slid his mouth away from her eagerly warm lips and pressed his face against her hair until his breathing slowed to an even, steady rhythm. 'Let's not do *that* again,' he whispered wryly as he laid his head against the pillow and closed his eyes to shut out the sight of her desire-clouded face. 'At least not tonight.'

'Ben . . .' She touched her fingers to his cheek, attempting with that touch to smooth away all of the old pains she didn't understand, but they were still there beneath her loving hand. 'I won't fight the song with an injunction. You can have the success you want so badly.' And she would give up hers. That was the unspoken knowledge that passed between them in one glance.

'Why?'

'Because I love you.' Her answer was the barest whisper, but he had heard it, and his eyes darkened with a renewed pain. He didn't feel the same miraculously dawning love that filled her with a strange new tenderness, she understood. But what he felt was more than simple physical desire. She could see that in his troubled face, and she could feel it in the arm that circled her shoulders to coax her down against him.

Ellie laid her head against the lean triangle of his shoulder and inhaled the musky sweetness of his skin. If nothing else, there was affection between them, and that was miracle enough for now. She stirred just enough to see his melancholy face, wondering how to end the sadness that seemed to have doubled with her words. 'You don't have to tell me that you love me, too,' she reassured him. 'I don't expect it.'

Ben's mouth quirked outward into a bitterly unhappy smile. 'Go to sleep, pretty lady,' he suggested evenly, stroking her hair with a gentle hand. 'And stop filling my ears with that lazy whisky voice of yours. Ssh,' he cautioned when she opened her mouth to give an answer. 'I'm only human, Ellie.'

CHAPTER SEVEN

'IN other entertainment news . . .' Ellie's eyes just brushed the printed page that lay on the desk in front of her before she faced the camera with a smile. 'The Denver Symphony Orchestra is playing a benefit performance here in Boulder Friday, Saturday and Sunday nights. They are always worth hearing, especially so now with their fine violin section. My weekend recommendation is . . .'

Ellie faltered for the barest moment as she glanced past the cameras and caught sight of a sheepskin jacket. Ben was back from the mountains! she realised, filled with an almost unbearable excitement at the prospect of being in his arms again. '. . . their children's matinee of *Peter and the Wolf*.' She forced her attention back to the work at hand. 'The rich, dramatic music of this perennial favourite will be augmented by the Boulder Dance Ensemble performing in full costume. The concert, scheduled for Sunday afternoon at one, is the perfect experience for anyone who loves both dance and music.'

'Sounds like a great place to take the kids,' Tim Blake, the show's anchorman, made friendly conversation as he gathered up the papers on his desk. 'Thank you, Eleanora. To recap our lead story tonight: it looks like the snowstorm that Jack predicted yesterday is going to swing east and miss the Boulder area after all. We will keep you updated on any further changes.'

Ellie waited only long enough to make sure the camera was off, then she slipped off her mike and laid it on the desk.

'Isn't that Ben Kolter?' Tim asked, frowning with concern as Ben stepped forward into the light. 'I can get security to toss him out.'

'No! No, no, I'll be fine,' Ellie reassured him quickly. The last thing on earth she wanted was to have Ben thrown out of the studio, but Tim's concern had suddenly reminded her that no one knew about her and the cowboy. Maybe it would be better that way. The newspapers would have a field day with the gossip.

'Miss Martin.' Ben smiled curtly as he stepped closer to the desk. 'I wonder if I could have a word with you? It's about business.

'Of course, Mr Kolter,' she greeted him with a civil nod, although she really wanted to fling her arms around him in an enthusiastic greeting. But she couldn't do that at the moment, not in front of Tim and the rest of the curious members of the crew. 'Why don't you come to my dressing-room? We can speak privately there.'

'All right.'

Ben followed her along the maze of corridors, his hands shoved into the pockets of his heavy sheepskin coat, but neither of them said a word until she had shut her dressing-room door behind them. Then she threw herself into his arms with all the pent-up longing she had felt for the past few days. 'I've missed you!'

'Save it, lady.' His voice was as harsh as the hand that stopped her and firmly pushed her back. 'If I wanted passion, I wouldn't come to you.'

'What?' She stared at him in hurt bewilderment.

'I came to ask you what the hell this is,' he demanded fiercely, pulling a legal document from his pocket and holding it in front of her.

For a moment Ellie was too surprised to speak. She took the paper from his hand and read through it quickly. Ben Kolter, the Travelling Asylum Band, and the Mountain West Recording Company were enjoined from distributing the record *Eleanora,* performing the song in concert, or using the song for any further commercial purposes until the courts had decided whether it infringed on Eleanora Martin's right to privacy.

'It's an injunction,' she said matter-of-factly, reading through the document again. She hadn't filed for it. This document had been filed by her father's lawyer. 'This is a mistake.'

'And I made it!' Ben snapped a cynical response. 'I should have known better than to believe someone like you. You're a spoiled, rich brat who doesn't know the first thing about being a woman!'

How could he say that to her after what had happened Christmas Eve? She had told him that she loved him. Did he think she said that to every man who wandered through her life?

'But you're going to tell me what it means

to be a woman, aren't you?' Ellie guessed sarcastically. 'I'll bet it has to do with sacrificing everything for you! *Your* song, *your* career, *your* damn whims!' she accused him as she pulled on her coat and found her bag. 'What about *my* career and *my* damn whims!'

'You made me a promise, and . . .'

'And I kept it!' she retorted, opening the door. 'My father filed for that injunction without telling me he planned to do it, and tomorrow morning I'll call his lawyer to have it rescinded. You could have given me the benefit of the doubt before you stormed in here to call me a two-faced hypocrite!' She slammed the door behind her to shut out the sight of his angry face. All she wanted was to get away from him and the furious accusations that proved he didn't care enough about her to accord her the smallest amount of trust.

'Ellie!' She wasn't at all surprised when she heard the door open and slam shut again. Then she heard the sound of footsteps behind her in the hall.

'I'll apologise,' he muttered. 'But you have to calm down and listen.' Ellie increased her pace until she was almost running through the hallways to the lobby. 'Damn it, Eleanora!' he called out behind her, but Ellie didn't stop. 'You're going to listen to me, if I have to drag you off and tie you up! Don't you walk away from me when I'm trying to have a conversation!' he demanded, catching up to her in the car park and seizing her wrist to stop her striding steps. 'Not after what happened between us on Christmas Eve.'

'You kissed me, and then we fell asleep on the couch. I don't think that changes anything between us,' lied Ellie, shaking his hand away. 'It certainly hasn't made you trust me. But it made me trust you,' she muttered, pulling out her keys and jamming one into the door lock of her car. 'I think that's what you intended all along.' She rattled the key, irritated that it wouldn't turn. 'I think you romanced me deliberately to make me drop the injunction against . . .'

For just a moment the truth was clear on Ben's tense, unhappy face, and she straightened up to meet his panicked eyes. 'My God,' she whispered hoarsely. 'I'm right, aren't I?'

A door had opened deep inside her and she fell into a deep abyss of pain. Everthing he'd done had been deliberate. She saw it all so clearly now. His tenderness, his arms, even his kiss on Christmas Eve, had all been part of a plot to make her change her mind. And she had been gullible enough to fall for it. If her father hadn't taken legal action she might never have known how dishonest the man was. But she certainly knew now.

'Ellie . . .'

'Don't you dare touch me again!' Ellie lashed out in wounded fury. Ben made no attempt to stop the palm that struck his cheek a resounding blow, but when she backed away he seized her arm and met her tear-filled eyes with the full weight of regret.

'You're right, Ellie,' he conceded painfully. 'But it's only half of the truth.'

'Is the other half as pleasant?' she demanded
bitterly, frightened by how easily his touch could
move her despite what she now knew.

'I don't supose it is,' he admitted tersely. 'But
you might as well hear it. Give me the keys,' he
demanded, taking the key chain from her
trembling hand and shaking it until he found the
car key. He unlocked the door and gestured
with a nod. 'Get in and slide over. And keep
your mouth shut,' he added, following her into
the car. 'It's hard enough for me to admit what
kind of man I am. I don't need you adding your
two cents' worth until I get my own thoughts
straight.

'Where are you taking me?' Ellie asked, rubbing
the steam away from the passenger window to
stare into the darkness. They had been driving
for an hour, and now they were climbing steadily
as Ben manoeuvred her car along a winding
mountain road.

'I'll have you back in time for work tomorrow.'
It wasn't an answer to her question, but it was
more than either of them had dared to say so
far. In the past half hour the wind had picked
up strength until it howled around them like a
banshee's keening wail, and there were sleety
snowflakes pelting down against the windscreen.
But Ellie settled back against the seat and pulled
her coat around her, strangely confident that she
was safe. Whatever Ben Kolter meant to do, she
was sure he wouldn't hurt her.

Finally the road levelled off, and a moment
later Ben stopped the car. 'When I open the

garage door, you drive in,' he ordered as he opened the car door.

He got out, hunching his neck down into his coat as he was hit by a howling blast of wind. He disappeared into the darkness, but by the time Ellie slid into the driver's seat, there was a square of light in front of her. She put the car in gear and drove it into the garage, parking it beside a pickup truck and a small grey sports car she could barely see beyond it.

Ben's cheeks were as red as a slap mark and snow dusted his dark hair, but he managed a weak smile as he closed the door behind them. 'Let's get inside and warm up,' he suggested, gesturing to a door that was set in a wall of solid rock. 'It's an old mine shaft,' he explained, reaching out to flick a switch that illuminated a tunnel through the rock. 'Left over from the goldmining days.' She moved instinctively closer, comforted by the hand that fell against her back to guide her through the tunnel.

There was another door at the far end of the tunnel, and Ben unlocked it, flicking on the light as he ushered her into an enormous room. It was the strangest house she'd ever seen, and one of the most beautiful. Three walls were mottled granite and the fourth was covered by an enormous woven tapestry of trees, the colours as vibrant as a fragrant summer's day.

'This is incredible!' Ellie whispered, glancing around her curiously. The house had been carved into the mountain. The floors were covered with plush carpeting and the walls were decorated with a wonderful conglomeration of eccentric artifacts. A framed collection of Indian arrowheads drew her attention for a moment, then she wove her way between the comfortable easy chairs to examine a mottled skull that hung above the mantel of the large fireplace.

'It's a fossilised hadrosaur skull,' Ben explained as he followed her progress around the enormous room. 'I've always liked dinosaurs,' he added a little sheepishly. 'Murphy says I stopped growing up when I reached twelve.'

Ellie had already wandered to the other end of the cavernous room, to a beautiful, modern kitchen, where she noted a vein of glittery yellow that wound a sinuous course along the mica-flecked grey granite of the wall. 'It's gold,' he confirmed her guess as she ran her finger along the vein of mustard-yellow rock. 'I bought this land from an old miner who never made a strike, and I found gold while I was blasting for the house. That's always been my kind of luck,' he admitted wryly. 'I go looking for one thing and I stumble over something else.'

His eyes met hers, and for a moment she wondered if he were referring to more than the vein of gold. He had gone looking for success and he had found her instead. 'Like the dinosaur skull,' he admitted as he glanced restlessly away. 'I was looking for turquoise when I found that. But that's not what I brought you here to see.'

He led her down a flight of stairs, past a large library and games room where the tapestry trees were blazing with the golds and reds of autumn. The walls were hung with paintings that were obviously expensive, and Ellie paused just long enough to try to frame a question.

'Does country music pay well?' she asked curiously. Murphy didn't live in this kind of luxury, although she supposed that supporting four ex-wives and six children might account for that.

'I inherited my money.'

'From your family?' It occurred to Ellie that she knew almost nothing about the man who had brought her here. She had fallen in love with him and didn't know the simplest of facts.

'From my family,' Ben echoed, so unhappily that Ellie almost asked another question but Ben turned away as if the subject had been closed. 'I want you to see something on the bottom floor.' She followed him down another flight of stairs and blinked in surprise when Ben flicked on the lights. This floor of the house was a rehearsal room complete with a sound-proofed recording booth and banks of complicated electronic gear. 'When we get the songs for the new album rehearsed, we'll move up here to do the recording,' Ben explained, parting the tapestry curtain of bare, winter trees to stare into the valley that stretched out below the house.

He hadn't brought her here to see the house or the recording room, Ellie understood as she noticed a set of cardboard panels that were propped along the wall. It was the storyboard for the video of *Eleanora,* she realised, stooping down to examine them more closely. In the first cartoon-like panel Ben turned on a television set and watched as Eleanora Martin gave her review of the Travelling Asylum Band.

'Ben Kolter's comeback performance could more aptly be described as a throwback performance . . .' Ellie winced as she read the words in the balloon above the character's head. Had she really been that cuttingly unkind?

In the second panel Ben had fallen asleep and the action cut to a dream sequence. A medieval princess on a horse was pursued by a band of barbarians dressed in ragged skins. She recognised Ben and Murphy and the others in the sketches, but every picture of the princess showed her from the back, and it wasn't difficult to realise what they meant to do. They were going to try to obtain the tapes of her review from the television station. Then they'd hire an actress with her general build and hair colour and interweave the scenes until it seemed that she was playing the role of the medieval princess.

But it wouldn't be easy to obtain the tapes if she objected, especially with an injunction hanging over everybody's heads. 'What are you going to do if the station manager says no to using the tapes?' Ellie asked Ben practically, meeting his brown eyes with a shrewd understanding of the way his mind worked. He had hedged his bets. She understood that now. 'You're going to use the Nashville tape instead, aren't you?' she guessed.

Ben's eyes fell restlessly away from hers, but he nodded yes.

'You planned it from the beginning,' she said evenly in a voice that held neither curiosity nor accusation. He had set out to get exactly what he wanted, and the passion he'd pretended had been nothing but an act.

But something had changed, she understood, studying his tense shoulders. He had set out to use her to satisfy his own ambitions and he had found himself caught up in far more complicated feelings.

'I'm a hustler, Ellie.' His answer was a whisper. 'I guess I always have been.'

Ellie balanced her chin against her knees to study his regretful face. She wished there was some way to compromise, some way for him to make the video without leaving her open to more ridicule. 'When I found you on that highway, I realised I had stumbled on to a major piece of luck,' Ben continued his confession as he pulled back the curtains again to look out at the cloud-veiled wintry moon. 'I wanted a piece of film that I could use for a video. Then I got even more ambitious. Why not romance the lady and talk her into doing the entire video? I overestimated my own attractiveness,' he admitted with a self-mocking smile. 'And I underestimated how much it would hurt if you slapped me down.

'When romancing you didn't work, I goaded you into a feud. It didn't matter what angle I played as long as I got the publicity I needed. I wanted to get the band back on top again, and I didn't care if I used you,' he admitted honestly. 'I had you pegged for a rich, spoiled snob who didn't have to work for what you wanted, so who was going to care if I took you down a notch?'

He wasn't entirely a hustler, Ellie thought, watching him as he stepped closer and crouched down to look at the cardboard panels. Ever since the beginning there had been a streak of concern and gentleness in Ben Kolter's nature. 'In my whole life I've only loved one person until . . .'

Until he had fallen in love with her? Ellie's heart stirred with an unexpected hope. Was that what the cowboy had brought her here to say? If that was it, he didn't say it.

'I don't expect you to like me very much right now,' he admitted as he picked up one of the cardboard panels and stared at it with eyes that were dark and grim. 'I don't even like myself. I wish I had never written that Godforsaken song,' he muttered harshly as he tossed the panel to the floor. 'You can have it, Ellie,' he offered unexpectedly. 'I won't sing it again, and I won't do the video. I'll even do what I can to get the remaining records off the market.'

'But you need it for the album,' she reminded him, astounded at what he was giving up. It was a sure shot at the top after ten years of obscurity. He'd told her that himself. 'You need it for the band's success.'

'Success isn't the most important thing in life,' he answered with a shrug. 'Didn't your daddy ever tell you that?' Then, because he seemed embarrassed by his own gesture of generosity, he flicked off the lights. 'Let's go upstairs and have a cup of coffee,' he suggested tersely. 'Then I'll drive you home.'

A warming blaze filled the fireplace and Ben sat on the couch, sipping a cup of coffee while he stared intently at the nervous tongues of flame. Outside, the wind had picked up again, lashing the house with icy hands, but no draught disturbed the curtains at the windows.

Did he love her? Ellie wondered as she wandered restlessly around the room, sipping her glass of brandy. Or was this just another trick? Had he told her everything because she was bound to find it all out eventually? He was a hustler who didn't care if she got hurt, but even as she thought that, she knew it wasn't true. His face was pale and moody, and his shoulders slumped as if he were resigned to his defeat. If he had used her to promote his own career, he had done it against a conscience that had tortured him with doubt until he had come to realise his mistake. He hadn't simply confessed to his manipulations. He had given them all up.

Where did that leave them? she wondered desperately, wishing there was a way to read his heart as clearly as she could read her own. She had loved the man despite the cautions of her common sense and reason, and now she loved him even more. Knowing how capable he was of deceiving her did nothing to lessen her desire.

Ellie touched her finger to the fossilised dinosaur skull above the mantel, imagining the moment that he had loosened the ancient fragment of life from the concealing earth. Then her attention was caught by a small picture in a silver frame.

It was Ben, with an adoring six-year-old clinging to his shoulders. Her eyes were dark like his, and a jet-black pigtail dangled teasingly in front of his face. At the moment that the photograph was taken he had opened his mouth to catch that pigtail in his teeth and the child had just erupted into a delighted laugh.

It was a charming picture, made even more so by the obvious exuberance of the love between Ben Kolter and the child. His child, Ellie knew as she took down the picture to examine it more closely. The dark, laughing eyes were just like his, and so were the finely moulded features of her face. 'What's her name?' she asked when she looked up to find Ben watching her.

'Becky.'

'Becky Kolter,' Ellie murmured with a smile. 'She's a beautiful little girl. Where is she now?'

'She's with her mother,' he answered, getting up so abruptly that Ellie was left to stare at the tense contours of his back. And her mother wasn't here, she could read the obvious in his evasive restlessness. His wife was the only person he had ever loved, but the marriage hadn't worked. It wasn't so terribly unusual, but she supposed it still must hurt.

'Do you play that, too?' she asked him when he stopped beside the piano and stared at it with weary sadness.

'Yes.'

'Will you play something for me?' Ellie asked, replacing the picture on the mantel. 'A Chopin nocturne,' she suggested in an effort to humour him into a less melancholy mood. 'Can you play Chopin with a country beat?'

'I'm afraid not.' He rewarded her teasing with a weakly grateful smile. Then he sat down and touched his fingers to the keys, coaxing out one clear, sweet note after the other until the room reverberated with the sound of a flawlessly perfect Chopin nocturne that left Ellie completely breathless. How many more times was Ben Kolter going to take her by surprise?

'Where did you learn to play like *that*?'

'In Paris,' Ben admitted as his fingers lingered on the keys. 'I had too much time and too much money, so I decided to put them both to use.'

In Paris? Ellie didn't have a chance to ask all the questions that suddenly filled her mind before he changed the subject. 'Do you play, Ellie?'

'Not like you do,' she admitted honestly. 'A little, though. My mother thought it was a vital part of a well-rounded education.'

'Good for her.' His lips were stretched outward into a soft, reflective smile as he coaxed out a melody that seemed as half-formed as a dream. 'I told Becky I'd sell her to the gypsies if she didn't learn to play.'

Ellie didn't believe him for a minute. She had seen him with Murphy's children and she knew his style: indulgence and persuasion mixed with a good dose of fun. 'Is she still in Paris?'

'Yeah.' Then, before she could ask another question, he nodded to the bench. 'Sit down and help me play.'

She set her brandy on the top of the piano

and sat down beside him. 'Play this,' he suggested, tapping out a tune. Ellie repeated the notes in a higher octave.

'It's pretty,' she admitted. 'What is it?'

'My baby left me and my cat is drunk . . .' He sang a teasing accompaniment to the lilting tune. 'My car was stolen and my rowboat sunk . . .' His voice trailed off with the last echo of the note. Then he chanced a sidelong glance at her curious face. 'Do you want to hear the real lyrics?'

'Yes.' She wanted that very much.

Ben put his fingers on the keys and played the tune again. 'The winds are cold in the high country . . . where a man grows bitter and grows old . . . I've spent my life in the high country . . . searching for shining streams of gold . . .'

His voice reverberated with a sensual energy as he sang the ballad of a miner who searched for gold and found love instead. It was a beautiful song, liltingly romantic and so softly stirring that Ellie felt a shiver in her spine as she listened to him play. It was one of the songs that he had talked about on Christmas Eve, one of the songs that people would hear if they bought his album. But, to ensure the success of the album, he needed to promote *Eleanora*.

' . . . Send the winds to the high country . . . I have no fear of the cold . . . My love's beside me in the high country . . . with hair like shining streams of gold . . .'

He had talent, Ellie understood as the music flowed around her, creating a longing, aching desire to know the warmth of his strong arms.

'My love's beside me in the . . .' His fingers accidentally touched her hand and his voice faltered for a moment. '. . . high country,' he finished in a whisper as his hand lingered, then folded around hers. 'Ellie . . .'

It was a question, and she gave her answer in a wordless look, breathlessly expectant as he coaxed her closer and met her mouth with a sweetly lingering kiss. 'Ellie . . .' Ben's mouth trailed across her cheek as if he sought to memorise the warmth of her soft flesh. 'You don't know how much I want to make love to you.'

'Yes, I do.' Her answer was a whisper as she put her arms around him. 'I want that just as much, Ben.'

She pressed her face against the triangle of his throat, inhaling the musky aroma of his skin as he lifted her in his arms and carried her upstairs. Then he laid her back against the pillows of his bed and met her mouth again with a possessive passion that sent her reeling through a universe of answering desire.

Again and again he kissed her until she was delirious with his touch. Then, when she was close to a mindless pleasure at the caresses that fell so hungrily against her upraised mouth, Ben pulled away.

'No . . .' Ellie moaned, reaching out to catch his sleeve.

'I'm adjusting the light, love,' he reassured her, turning the lamp on his dresser until the room was bathed in a subdued, romantic light. He smiled as he stood at the foot of the bed, unbuttoning his cuffs. A moment later he unbuttoned his cotton shirt and slid it from his shoulders.

His shoulders were broad and muscular, his chest just lightly covered with a triangle of soft brown hair against which hung a golden talisman that reflected a quick burst of light. When he undid his belt and put his hands against his jeans, Ellie glanced modestly away.

'Look at me.' His voice was deep and commanding, and she obeyed, revelling in the beauty of his powerful, lean body as he came around the bed.

'There's something I've wanted to do since the first moment I laid eyes on you, Eleanora,' Ben whispered as he put his arms around her and pulled her up beside him. He reached behind her and pulled out a hairpin. Another followed, then another, and her blonde hair cascaded across her shoulders like water tumbling to a mountain pool. 'You're the most beautiful woman I've ever seen. Do you know that?' he asked as his hand fanned out against the nape of her neck to hold her still beneath the warmth of his caress.

'Yes.' She gave him the answer she knew he wanted. And she believed it, she realised, losing herself in the appreciation of his brown-eyed gaze. She was beautiful in Ben Kolter's eyes, and this very moment there was no universe beyond the boundary of his eyes and hands and mouth.

Ben unbottoned her blouse and pushed it from her shoulders, undressing her with the same slow care he had shown the night that she was drunk. But now, when she lay naked, he stretched himself beside her and bent down to kiss her upraised nipples with torturously slow strokes.

'I've waited for a long time, Ellie. I can wait until you're ready.' He met her mouth again, entreatingly gentle, raising her to the brink of a trembling desire to know the power of love. Then, with the most exquisite care, he carried her across that brink and made her his completely.

CHAPTER EIGHT

'BEN . . .' Ellie stumbled blindly through the snow, clawing the air in front of her in an attempt to find an anchor in the howling wind that propelled her forward. 'Ben?' she screamed, losing her balance on the shifting mountain surface. Then, just as she was about to plunge over the edge of an icy cliff into a dark abyss, an arm circled her and dragged her back into the dimly lit comfort of a cave.

Outside, a band of wolves howled a blood-curdling threat that drove her deeper into the encircling arms that promised her protection. 'Save me from the wolves,' she pleaded sleepily, pressing her face to the fragrant warmth of a down-covered chest. 'Don't let them in here.'

'It's too late,' a lazy voice drawled back. 'You're in bed with one already.'

It had been a dream, she understood, smiling with relief as a hand stroked down her back in an unhurried exploration. There were no wolves, Just wind, screaming its way between the mountains as if it were in pain. She was safe here in a cave of downy quilts, bending her lithe body to the contours of Ben's chest and legs.

She lifted her head just enough to meet his half-open eyes. 'You're not a wolf,' she murmured teasingly, pushing herself up on her elbow until she could meet his mouth with a flirtatious good-morning kiss. 'You're a pussycat.'

'Pussycat?' His arms tightened around her to hold her to his chest. 'You dare to call Ben Kolter a pussycat? Do you know what I'm going to do to you?'

She knew what she wanted him to do as he rolled her over against the pillows and pinned her shoulders down, but he was grinning too mischievously. He flicked out his tongue to lightly touch her nose. 'No!' Ellie giggled, struggling to break free as he smoothed a path across her cheek and darted his tongue into her ear. 'Don't lick me!' she pleaded breathlessly. 'I'm sorry I called you a pussycat!' But Ben had already moved down to her breast and his tongue created a fierce wave of longing as it circled her firm nipple in determinedly teasing strokes.

'Oh . . .' Ellie moaned with pleasure. 'You're not going to teach me a lesson this way! You know that, don't you?' Her fingers wove through his hair, clutching him to her in a frenzy of desire as his thighs touched hers, his greater weight lying easily against her.

'Isn't this the way to tame a wildcat?' Ben asked as he braced his arms beside her shoulders to take his weight and bent down to touch his lips to hers with a seductive stroke.

'Yes.' Her answer was a breath that he inhaled as he deepened his possession. She was his to command and lead, his to hold with an insistent passion that extinguished all her thoughts except for the pleasure of his masculine, sweet touch.

She ached with a physical desire that peaked
and peaked again until she felt that she would
burst apart with an exultant rapture in his arms.
'My God, you're beautiful . . .' Ben's voice was
a rasping whisper beside her ear as he pressed
his face against her silken, unloosed hair and let
his breathing slow to a more even rhythm. 'So
beautiful . . .' he repeated as his lips touched
her cheek and lingered there in an affectionately
soft touch.

'You're not so bad yourself, cowboy,' she
returned the compliment, turning her face against
the pillow until she could meet his luminescently
warm eyes. She was in love with the man. He
was the worst possible man to fall in love with,
but she had already learned that love made little
sense.

'So . . .' Ben's fingers lightly grazed her pink,
flushed cheek. 'Where's my breakfast, wench?'
He pressed his thumb against her lips to stop
her snapped reply. 'That was a joke, love. I'm
going to get up and make you the best pancakes
that can be made with powdered milk.'

He lightly kissed her nose, then pushed back
the covers and stepped out of bed, letting out a
curse as his warm body came in contact with the
air. 'God almighty, it's freezing in here,' he
muttered, opening his cupboard to find a terry
cloth robe. Then he adjusted the thermostat
beside the door, frowning as he cocked his head
to listen for the click of the furnace coming on.
He pushed the button for the light, but absolutely
nothing happened.

'The electricity's out.' Ben's voice sounded

bewildered more than worried. Ellie watched him curiously as he strode to the window and pulled back the curtains. He gave a low whistle of surprise. 'Remember that storm that was supposed to miss us? Take a look at this.' He pulled the draperies aside, leaving Ellie to stare in wonderment at a thick fog of swirling snow.

'It's beautiful!'

'I'm glad you think so, love.' Her response amused him. 'Because we're not getting off this mountain today. Not in a white-out like this.'

'Oh.' She understood. They were marooned here until the storm was over. Maybe even longer. The mountain road that led up here wouldn't be the first one to be ploughed. 'I have to work tonight. I've never missed a day of work in my life.'

'There's always a first time,' Ben said philosophically as he picked up the phone and set it on the bed beside her. 'Call the station and tell them that you'll be in to work as soon as the Saint Bernards find us. I'm going to get a fire going and make us some coffee.'

'Guess what else is out,' Ellie greeted Ben as she came down the stairway from the bedroom wrapped in a quilt that trailed behind her like the train of a bridal gown.

'The phone, too?' Ben frowned as he looked up from the gas stove where he was making pancakes. 'They're probably going to think I kidnapped you,' he joked, lifting a pot from the back burner and pouring her a cup of hot, black coffee. 'There *is* a bright side to this disaster. At least you're marooned with the most fascinating man in the country.'

'If not the most modest,' Ellie laughed. She worried a little bit about what would happen when she didn't show up at the station, but she was far more concerned about the fact that she didn't worry more. When Ben glanced at her with his luminously warm eyes, she didn't think about anything but him.

Ben filled two plates with panckes and carried them to the living-room where he had made a blazing fire. Then he returned for the pot of coffee and the cups, grinning as the quilt slipped down from Ellie's naked breasts and she clutched it clumsily to pull it up. 'I have some clothes that might fit you,' he offered, setting the cups down on the fire-warmed hearth and holding out his hand to pull her down beside him on the rug. 'Although I rather like you in this get-up.'

'Did your ex-wife leave her clothes here when you were divorced?' she asked curiously as she balanced her plate on her lap and sliced into the pancakes.

'No,' he answered tersely. 'I was thinking of some of my clothes.' He was silent for a moment, then he frowned down at his plate. 'My wife and I weren't divorced, Ellie, That's not how our marriage ended.'

'How else could it have . . . Oh.' She understood. His wife had died. 'I'm sorry,' she said honestly. 'Was it an accident of some kind?'

'Not exactly.' He stabbed his fork into his pancakes and moved them across the plate. 'She kiiled herself,' he confessed. 'Maybe it was an accident. I don't know.'

'Oh,' Ellie answered once again, not knowing quite what to make of his hard-jawed matter-of-factness about the matter. But Ben didn't seem to expect any clichéd expression of sympathy for a woman she had never met. She met Ben's eyes with a reassuring smile, encouraging him to continue. 'You must have loved her very much.'

Ben leaned back against the sofa and stretched his feet towards the warming fire, staring at the flickering flames as if he understood their restless nervousness. 'I suppose I did at first,' he answered. 'I thought I did.'

His mouth turned downwards into a frown that etched lines of old pain at the corners if his lips, and he was silent for so long that Ellie was afraid he'd retreated into a private pain that he couldn't find the strength to share. But finally he stirred. 'Have you ever been to Telluride?' he asked her unexpectedly.

'Sure. My father has a condominium at one of the ski resorts there.'

'Well, I was born there,' Ben volunteered. 'Back before the ski resorts and the condominiums and the trendy people came—back when Telluride was full of dirt-poor people, and the Kolters were the poorest of the lot. My father ran off before I even know him, and my mother eventually drank herself to death. I didn't have a family, or an education, or anything else that might have made a difference. All I had was a face that women found attractive and a passable ability to make music.'

It was more than passble, thought Ellie, but she didn't interrupt him.

'Murphy and I figured singing was better than working for a living,' he continued wryly. 'So we put together a band and hit the road. We played forty weeks a year in every roadhouse and bar from here to Baltimore, and to our surprise we got pretty good.

'Then one night I looked out into the audience and I saw Laura Dunmore. I could tell that this lady had been raised a long way across the other side of the tracks from Telluride, Colorado. And I could tell that the lady wanted me. She was slumming, of course,' he admitted as he swallowed the remaining coffee in his cup and stood up to pour himself another. 'She was looking for a whole new set of kicks, and I was that month's grand adventure. But I didn't know that. I was still naïve enough to think a lady like her could love a man like me.'

'We were drunk when we got married, and when we finally sobered up Laura announced that she was going back to Europe. I could choose between her and the band, she told me. And, by the way, she thought she might be pregnant, but if I didn't want the hassle she'd take care of it.'

'You wanted the hassle,' Ellie guessed, not at all surprised when Ben nodded his agreement. He had left his band and friends to be with the woman he loved and the baby they had created.

'Then it all went from bad to worse,' Ben continued with the story. 'There was always someone—a race car driver or a tennis star or a . . .' he faltered momentarily '. . . or God knows who else. Laura could always find someone more exciting than her husband. But I stayed with her.'

'Because you still loved her,' Ellie prompted in the silence.

'No.' Ben's voice was flat and lifeless. 'I stopped loving Laura when I realised what kind of woman she really was. But I loved my kid.' He drained half the cup in one long swallow before he dared to meet Ellie's sympathetic eyes. 'It's funny, isn't it?' he asked. 'That selfish, self-absorbed woman gave me something so incredibly priceless that I . . .' His voice trailed off into a whisper that was so filled with emotion that Ellie looked away, embarrassed to be witnessing his pain.

'I stayed with Laura because that was the only way I could be with Becky, and I was willing to pay the price. I overlooked her interest in other men, and she realised pretty quickly that the arrangement could be convenient. As long as she was married, she wasn't apt to be trapped so easily again. It was a very fashionable marriage,' Ben smiled bitterly, 'and Laura prided herself on being a very fashionable woman. Unfortunately, I wasn't as willing to be fashionable about things that affected Becky. We were in Cannes for the winter season and Laura took up with a group of people who were doing drugs—cocaine, mostly—and that was the last straw for me. We fought about it, and when I couldn't make her come to her senses, I filed for custody of Becky.'

'But you didn't get it?' Ellie guessed.

'I did get it,' he disagreed. 'And the day I got it, Laura ran her car headlong into the side of a factory building outside of Cannes. The police estimate that she was doing eighty and was so high she didn't even see it coming .'

'And Becky . . .' She knew the answer the moment that she said the name. Ben's face was so tense and anguished it seemed carved from the grey granite of the Colorado mountains. 'She wasn't in the car?' Ellie cried the words. Ben barely nodded before he raised the cup and drained it dry.

'Oh, God . . .' She rested her face against her bent up knees and took a breath to stop her futile cry. She saw the child's face in her mind, laughing as she clung to her father's shoulders. But no matter how she tried, she couldn't shake another sight—a shattered, twisted car and a child-sized coffin. She knew Ben was thinking of those, too. 'She didn't do it deliberately—did she?'

'I don't know,' he answered wearily as he set his empty coffee cup down on the table. 'I don't know why Laura did anything she did. We were still legally married, so I inherited Laura's estate, but I'd give all that money away without a second thoguht if I could go back and change just one decision. If I hadn't waited for the court order, maybe Becky would still be . . .'

'It's not your fault!' Ellie interrupted before he could go on torturing himself with recriminations. 'You did what you thought was right. You didn't kill your daughter! Don't stay over there on the other side of the room, Ben,' she pleaded. 'Come here where I can see your face.'

'It's not much of a face right now.' He turned just enough for her to see the tears that etched their way across his tanned and handsome features, but when she held out her hand he came and let her coax his head down to her lap.

'It's not a bad face,' she said softly, smoothing her thumb across it with a reassuring stroke. No wonder he was bitter. He'd lost the child he had adored. And he'd lost her in a stupid, senseless way.

Ben inhaled a breath and attempted a weak smile. 'I came back here because the only time that I was ever really happy without . . . without Becky,' his voice faltered for only a bare second before he went on in a firmer voice, '. . . was with the band. And I owed Murphy something for walking out on him when we had a chance at real success. I wanted to get back on top again to erase everything that had happened, and I didn't care who I used to get there.'

'Especially a rich, spoiled brat like Laura,' Ellie guessed, understanding his hatred now. She had reminded him of the woman who had taken away his career and his child and torn his heart in two.

'Yes,' he admitted, turning his head enough to meet her sad green eyes. 'I wanted to flail out against all the rich, selfish bitches in this world because the one who had hurt me was beyond my reach. But I was wrong about you, Ellie. And about myself,' he added wearily. 'I never expected to care about you like I do.'

'I care about you, too, Ben.'

'I know,' he answered painfully. 'But I'm old enough to know the odds against it lasting. Not even Murphy can keep a relationship together on the road. Do you understand what I'm saying, Ellie?'

There was no future for them. She read that in the sharp unhappiness of his dark eyes. 'Yes,' she answered in a whisper, bending down to touch her mouth to his. If there was no future, at least they had a present filled with the unexpected gifts of sympathy and passion.

She'd feel the pain of parting when she had to feel it, she decided, meeting his eyes with a reassuring smile. Right now she'd revel in the time the storm had given them to be together in this mountain stronghold far from the world outside. 'I'm not looking for a relationship with a crazy cowboy,' Ellie attempted to humour him with her lie, 'I just came here for the pancakes.'

CHAPTER NINE

THE view from the kitchen window was spectacular. A wide, virgin valley spread out beneath the house, and then the landscape rose again into jagged mountain peaks that kissed the violet-grey morning sky. Two days of snow had covered everything with a pristine blanket, a new slate on which would be recorded every Y-shaped track of an alighting bird, every coat of snow shrugged off by the soaring fir trees as they warmed themselves in the pale, wintry sun.

It had already been etched with cross-country ski tracks that wound through the apple orchard and across the meadow, where Ben told Ellie deer would come to graze when the snows had been transformed into the fragile flowers of a mountain spring.

She loved it here, Ellie thought, staring out at the vista which as yet was barely touched by the promise of the dawn. She had loved the exhilaration of their skiing expedition when the storm had finally blown its vengeance out against the craggy peaks. They had sailed through the cloudless, velvet night, drenched in a golden wash of moonlight. Then they had returned to the house and made love in front of the blazing fire. Ellie could still feel the softness of the rug underneath her shoulders as Ben coaxed her back and met her mouth with his.

There was no future for them, but the present was enough, Ellie tried to convince herself as the first rays of sun iced the farthest mountain peaks with a blushing pink. But there was very little present left. She could feel it ebbing away from her like the darkness that retreated before the encroaching sunlight of the day. The storm had ended, and Ben had had a reason for suggesting that they ski.

'You handle yourself well on the downhills,' he had complimented when she had swooshed to a stop beside him. 'Do you think you could make an eight-mile trek tomorrow?'

They were going to ski down to the nearest village and find a ride to Boulder. Then the future would fall between them like a fog through which they would never again see each other with the same clarity of passion that seemed so real here in the mountains. Ben had his music and she had her job at the television station. Her career, she thought morosely, wondering why that word sounded so cold and distant now.

She couldn't hold her career in her arms and gaze into its laughingly warm eyes. Nor could she lose herself in it so completely that the reality of life stepped back to let the pure, undistilled essence of happiness hold sway.

For one short moment in Ben's arms she had understood the power of love fully felt, and she had tried to form the words she'd have to say. I would give up everything for you. She said them to herself now, wondering what Ben would have said if she had found the courage to murmur them out loud.

He wouldn't let her make a sacrifice like that to get so little in return. He had already told her that his career was the only thing that really mattered in his life. Now that Becky was gone, no one could compete with the compelling mistress of his music.

He had never promised anything except desire, Ellie reminded herself realistically. But he had given her affection as well as a passionate excitement that had burst like an explosive charge across the horizon of her life.

They still had a little time left, a few short hours before they would strap on their skis and make their careful way down the mountain road, and Ellie intended to make them as wonderful as Ben had made the past few days. She took the coffee cake she had made out of the oven and set it on the tray beside the coffee pot and cups. Then she set the tray against her hip and carried it upstairs to the bedroom, where she set it on the floor beside the bed.

Ben still lay there in his bed, his arm flung out against her pillow as if he had reached for her in his morning dreams. 'Benjamin,' Ellie whispered seductively against his ear. 'Are you going to sleep all day?'

'Hm?' He gave a groggy answer as he turned his head against the pillow. Then he squinted his eyes open to note the pearly luminescence of the dawn. 'What are *you* doing up at this hour?' he asked her affectionately, reaching up to touch his fingers to her smiling face.

'Planning surprises,' she admitted honestly. 'Close your eyes again. And open your mouth.'

'Uh-oh,' he answered with a grin. 'The last time I did this, Steven stuck a bug in my mouth.' But he trustingly closed his eyes and laid his head back on the pillow, opening his mouth when she ran her fingertip sensuously across his lower lip. She dipped the forefinger of her other hand into the apple-brandy topping of the cake and touched it to his tongue.

'Hm.' His lips closed around her finger.

'Do you like the topping?'

'No. I like your finger.' He seized her wrist and held it, running his tongue along her palm until she giggled like a schoolgirl. Then he met her laughing eyes, examining her flushed face and the tumbled hair that lay across her shoulders with such appreciation that Ellie glanced away with giddy pleasure. 'You're a very sexy lady, Eleanora,' he whispered hoarsely. 'Do you know that?'

'Sometimes I know that,' she admitted. When she was with him, she felt attractive and alive. 'I've made you breakfast.' She gestured to the tray that lay beside her on the floor. 'Coffee cake. We should eat it while it's hot.'

'We should do something else while *I'm* hot.'

'You don't cool off as quickly as coffee cake does,' Ellie answered with a laugh as she poured Ben a cup of coffee. 'Sit up and give me room to put the plates down on the bed.'

'You're sexy,' he repeated as he sat up against the headboard and smoothed the blankets flat. 'Bright, gorgeous, ambitious . . .'

'Well-dressed,' she added teasingly, turning

around to model the oversized velour robe she had taken from his closet. 'How do you like it?'

'I never see your clothes. I look right through them to what's underneath.' Whether he meant her body or her higher virtues he left her to imagine, although the deep brown eyes that met her accusing stare were not innocent at all. 'Come join me on the bed, little girl,' he suggested evenly. 'The big, bad wolf wants to talk to you.'

'About what?' She joined him on the bed, folding her legs to sit cross-legged beside him as he sipped his coffee.

'About you and me and the rest of the world. What are we going to do when we get back to Boulder?'

'I don't know.' She curled her fingers around her coffee cup to fight back a melancholy chill. She had forgotten everybody else.

'When we get to the bottom of the mountain, you could go on to Boulder by yourself,' Ben suggested evenly. 'No one has to know where you've spent the past few days. If we go back together . . . Well,' he sighed wearily as he cut a piece of cake. 'The press would have a field day with the gossip.'

He was right, of course. They had attracted so much attention with their feud that the papers would seize on any hint that the two of them were lovers. 'I could go back alone, and then later . . .' She already knew his answer from the pained look that crossed his face like a shadow that sailed across the sun. He was suggesting that they end it now before the maliciousness of gossip hurt her even more than he already had.

He was a very sweet man, Ellie thought, setting her coffee cup down on the bedside table. 'All right,' she agreed, leaning back against the pillows. She would walk away without giving him the complication of her tears, but she wouldn't leave before she told him what the past few days had meant.

'I don't regret anything that's happened between us, Ben. You've been a very good lover. And you've been a very good friend, too.'

'Thank you.' His answer was a whisper, and for one short moment she wondered if he was going to cry. But he inhaled a breath and met her eyes with a regretful smile. 'I like you, lady.'

'Do you, cowboy?' she answered, circling his shoulders with her arms. They still had time before they had to leave, and Ellie knew exactly how she wanted to spend it. 'You wouldn't want to prove that, would you?'

'Yes, ma'am.' His mouth quirked outward into a ready grin. Then he met her mouth with such an explosion of desire that Ellie sucked in an involuntary breath. His fingers twined through her yellow hair, holding her to him with such fierceness that she could feel the aching hunger in his heart, and when he pushed her back against the pillows she fell with him farther beyond the boundaries of passion than they had ever been before.

'You have a wonderfully responsive body,' Ben murmured appreciatively as his hand slipped past the neckline of her robe to find her upraised nipple. 'I'm surprised you don't have men beating down your door.'

'Who says I don't?' she challenged. 'I have so many men I can barely . . .'

Ben's face tensed so suddenly that Ellie stopped her teasing retort. He withdrew his hand and sat up, cocking his head as if he were listening to a far-off sound she couldn't hear.

'What's wrong?' she asked, alarmed. She pulled her robe closed and sat up beside him. She could hear the sound now, too, the low rustle of a pair of boots shuffling across a carpet.

'Someone's in the house.'

He had barely said the words when the bedroom door flew open. 'Freeze!'

'Good God!' Ben cried, stretching his arm out automatically to push Ellie behind him as he stared into the barrel of a gun.

'Put your hands up,' a state policeman ordered. 'And let the girl go.'

'What in the name of . . .'

'Let the girl go,' the officer repeated in such a tensely nervous voice that Ben put his arms up in the air and gestured with his head.

'Get off the bed, Ellie.'

'I don't understand what's happening. What have you . . .'

'Go!' Ben snapped tersely. 'Ask your questions later.'

Ellie scrambled off the bed, tightening the belt of her bathrobe with a hasty hand. 'What has he done?' she demanded. Three more policemen crowded through the bedroom door.

'He's wanted on a kidnapping charge. Are you Eleanora Martin?'

'Yes, but . . .'

'Did this man hurt you?' the policeman demanded, still aiming his gun dead centre at Ben Kolter's chest.

'No!' she said incredulously. 'And he didn't kidnap me, either, if that's what this thing is all about.'

'You haven't been kidnapped?' The officer lowered his gun just slightly.

'No! Put that thing away before you hurt somebody,' Ellie ordered snappishly.

To her surprise, the officer put on the safety catch and slipped the gun back into his holster, smiling apologetically at Ben. 'Sorry. You can put your hands down if you want.'

'Thanks.' Ben let out a breath of pure relief, but his reaction was short-lived. A photographer appeared in the doorway and raised his camera to photograph the bathrobe-clad woman and the man who sat in bed behind her.

Ellie was too confused to realise what was happening, but Ben reacted instantly. 'No!' he shouted in outrage. He jumped off the bed and was half-way across the room before Ellie and the officer could stop him. The flash went off again.

'Get him out of here!' Ben roared. 'This is private. I don't want this in the papers!'

'Calm down, Ben,' Ellie pleaded. 'You *are* going to be charged with a crime if you hit him.'

'Get him out of my house!' Ben ordered in a voice so fierce and angry that the photographer stepped back into the hallway, although he raised his camera once again. 'He's going to turn this into a public scandal! Oh, God, Ellie, I'm sorry . . .'

'Get him out of the house.' The officer snapped a terse command. He waited only long enough for a policeman to pull the photographer back along the hallway, then he shut the door and released his hold against the angry man.

'Thank you,' Ben whispered in a shaky voice, reaching out a protective arm for Ellie. 'I'm sorry that happened, love,' he said regretfully. 'It's going to make the papers now. It's all going to make the papers.'

'It's all right,' she reassured him, frightened by the pallor of his face and the way he balled his fingers into fists to keep his hands from shaking. 'Calm down, Ben,' she whispered, touching his cold face. 'It wasn't your fault.'

'Well, this is a fair mess, isn't it?' the state trooper said, gesturing to the breakfast tray that had been scattered across the bed. 'We had paperwork for a search and seizure, by the way. We had reason to believe that Miss Martin had been the victim of foul play.'

The mess wasn't *his* fault, Ellie mentally translated the trooper's careful words. They had reason to believe that she'd been kidnapped, and they'd burst into Ben Kolter's house in an attempt to save her life. She supposed she should be grateful.

'There's coffee downstairs in the kitchen,' she suggested, making an attempt to calm herself, although her heart was beating like a drum. 'Why don't your men go down and have a cup. We'll join you as soon as we're dressed.'

'That's most kind of you, Miss Martin.' The officer was pleased. 'You know,' he stopped just as he reached the door, 'my wife watches you all the time on the TV. I'll have to tell her that you're even prettier in person!'

'It's one of those cases where all the evidence added up to one conclusion.' Trooper Daniels sipped his coffee as he held forth at the kitchen table. 'There were all the threats that Kolter made: "Maybe I should drag her off . . ." "If I had one night alone with her, I could change her mind . . ." "I'm going to kill the lying bitch . . .'"

'Oh, God,' Ben closed his eyes and moaned.

'When did you say *that*?' Ellie demanded in surprise.

'When I was served with the injunction.'

'That's right,' Daniels added cheerfully. 'The injunction was a motive. The last time anyone saw you, Kolter was chasing you through the television station, screaming at you. Your dressing-room showed signs of a struggle, and the crumpled up injunction was lying on the floor. But it was your not showing up for work that made everyone suspicious. According to the station manager, it was inconceivable that you would fail to come to work, or at least get to a phone and call in. That's when they asked the state police to start an investigation.'

'The newspapers have been full of the story for days,' another trooper interjected, helping himself to a second cup of coffee. 'Your father flew into town the night before last on a private plane and the first thing he did was offer a fat reward for your safe return. I'm surprised we got here before you were over-run by fortune-hunters on snowmobiles.'

'The helicopter helped,' Daniels offered. 'It's going to be a week before you get your road ploughed out.'

Her father had come back, Ellie realised with surprise. She had forgotten all about him.

'We haven't seen a newspaper,' Ben answered evenly, reaching out unconsciously to circle Ellie's waist. 'It's hard to get delivery when the roads are impassable.'

'It's been on the television, too.'

'No electricity,' Ben said. 'No radio, no phone. I brought Ellie up here to show her the house, and we got marooned when the snowstorm hit. We were just trying to stay warm and comfortable until we could get back down the mountain.'

'Ah.' Trooper Daniels grinned. 'Well, that's certainly your own private business,' he admitted good-naturedly.

He was wrong about that, Ellie thought. Right now there was nothing in the world that was less their own private business than how the two of them had managed to stay warm and comfortable in the middle of the blizzard. The effects of a video of *Eleanora* would have been minor compared to the notoriety she and Ben would endure the minute that those photographs were published. And there was nothing she could do to stop it.

As if he read her thoughts, Ben stroked his thumb distractedly across her hand and met her eyes with a painfully regretful smile.

'I wonder,' Trooper Daniels said, pulling a notepad from his pocket, 'could I have your autographs for my wife? She loves both of you.'

CHAPTER TEN

'ELLIE?' It was Sara-Jean's soft voice that stopped her half-way up the stairs. 'I called the station, but they said you'd already left,' the young woman said timidly, as if she was apologising for bothering her at all. She had spoken to Ellie that way all week, and Ellie understood instinctively what Sara-Jean was feeling.

They were two women living in the same house, and they both moved carefully, carrying themselves like bowls that might spill too much emotion if either of them knocked too abruptly against the other.

'I took some messages for you while you were out,' Sara-Jean explained, handing her a stack of papers. 'Most of them are from magazines wanting you to do interviews, and I told them you'd get back to them if you were interested.'

'Thank you.' Ellie sorted through them quickly. There were messages from *People* and *McCall's*.

'And Ben called,' Sara-Jean added as Ellie turned to leave. 'He has your car at Sloan Murphy's ranch.' Ben was back in Boulder! The very thought made Ellie's heart quicken with the expectation that she'd be in his arms again. 'I'd be happy to drive you over there,' added Sara-Jean hopefully.

'No, that's all right,' Ellie answered. 'I can take a cab.'

'Of course.' Sara-Jean smiled bravely, but Ellie could see the hurt in the woman's eyes, a hurt that she'd inflicted tactlessly. Sara-Jean was trying to be friendly. What would it hurt for her to try as well?

'I'm sorry you had to come back to Boulder,' Ellie said, groaning at the words the moment they had left her mouth. 'I didn't mean it that way,' she corrected quickly. 'I mean, I'm sorry that I was responsible for ruining your honeymoon. But . . .' she faltered as she met Sara-Jean's brown eyes. 'But thank you,' she went on. 'I know it was your idea to return when you thought that I'd been kidnapped.'

'It wasn't,' Sara-Jean said earnestly. 'I would have suggested it, but your father had already made the decision by the time he talked to me. He made it while he was still on the phone with the police.'

Maybe that was the truth, Ellie thought, studying the woman's face. And maybe it wasn't. All she knew for certain was that Sara-Jean was kind and gracious. All the anger that Ellie had felt towards her had been totally misplaced. 'Thank you,' she murmured. 'Are you sure it wouldn't be too much trouble for you to drive me out to Bendix Road?'

'No.' Sara-Jean's eyes brightened with an unexpectedly grateful light. 'It won't be any trouble at all.'

'The driveway's up here on the left,' Ellie

directed as Sara-Jean manoeuvred her small sedan along the road. She didn't bother to hide her smile of flushed excitement as they turned up the road and approached the house. It had been eight days since she had left Ben's house and returned to Boulder in the state police helicopter, eight days that seemed like years of longing for his arms. Now that she was here, Ellie was filled with giddy excitement. 'Do you think he'll like my new hairdo?' she asked, running an anxious hand across the yellow curls that cascaded from beneath her peacock blue knit cap.

'I think you could shave yourself bald and he'd still like the way you look,' Sara-Jean reassured her, 'and I don't have to ask how you feel about him,' she laughed as she reached across to open Ellie's door. 'Go and show him your new hairdo.'

She waited until Ellie had closed the car door behind her, then she gave a cheerful wave and turned the car around to head back to the highway. Ellie was already on the porch. No one answered her knock, so she opened the front door and slipped into the hallway, following the sound of music to a room at the far end of the house.

'Give me a two-count before you come in, Trawler.' It was Ben Kolter's voice, clear and even, that spoke above the strident notes of a guitar. 'After I sing, "You must have known I wouldn't stay," wait. One. Two. Then give me a good downbeat to seque into the chorus. That's when you come in, Murphy. On "I love you in a cowboy's sometime way."'

'Got it.'

'Okay, let's take it from the top,' Ben suggested, raking his fingers quickly across the strings of his guitar. 'It's been a sweet time, darling, since I found your door . . . But everyone has got a price to pay . . . All the time you dreamed about tomorrow . . . You must have known I wouldn't stay . . .'

Ellie leaned against the door frame, watching the band at work. Trawler half-closed his eyes as he beat on the drums, and Ben leaned over his guitar, playing it as if the country music flowed from his soul instead of from a wooden echo chamber topped by a set of strings. 'I loved you in a cowboy's sometime way . . . I loved you as a pine tree loves a summer's day . . . I loved you as a sailboat loves a sheltered bay . . . In my sometime . . . goodtime . . . cowboy way . . .'

The guitar music quickened, and the drum beat an answering tattoo. The music surged upward with a boisterous enthusiasm, then all four voices joined to sing the chorus, bringing the song to a rowdy, crashing finale. 'Whoa!' Murphy laughed, using the back of his hand to wipe the sweat away from his broad forehead. 'What's your girlfriend going to say about that one, Ben?'

'Are you asking for a professional critique?' Ellie responded, smiling when Ben turned around to regard her with a mixture of surprise and open admiration.

She wore a steel-blue ski parka over a pair of jeans, but the most startling change about her was the halo of loose blonde hair that curled against her shoulders. It had been a whim to have her hair done, but she could gauge the effect of the new hairstyle in the appreciative mirror of Ben's eyes. 'The song exemplifies Ben Kolter's personal style,' she said teasingly, as she crossed the room. 'Its words are simple and self-mocking, but the melody is bursting with the virile, kinetic energy that is a hallmark of the West itself.'

'What did she say?' Murphy demanded as Ben's arms folded around her in an affectionately warm caress.

'The lady likes it,' she answered with a laugh.

'So does the cowboy.' Ben's fingers touched her hair. 'Did you come out here to get your pretty little car back before I get too fond of it?'

'Not entirely,' she admitted. She disentangled herself from Ben's arms and opened her bag to pull out a magazine. 'We've made *Time* magazine. Shall I read you this jounalistic gem?'

'*Time* magazine?' Ben winced. '*The Time* magazine?'

'Yep.' She opened it to the page that she had marked and read the headline above the story. '"The Saga of the Cowboy and the Lady.

"For months now the residents of the Rocky Mountain area have been entertained by the open feuding between a romantically attractive country-western singer and a honey-voiced reporter for station WQBX in Boulder, Colorado. She suggested that he do the music world a favour by making his comeback concert a farewell performance. He responded with a wickedly witty song suggesting that the male members of her audience might be tuning in for reasons other than her thought-provoking assessments of Boulder's cultural events. 'The iceberg has a damn nice body', he has been quoted as saying. 'I'd like to show her what to do with it'.

"Through it all, Eleanora Martin has maintained a regally professional demeanour and a frank disdain for Ben Kolter's 'tuneless cacophonies and pathetically inane lyrics'. How to explain, then, her sudden disappearance on the day she slapped an injunction on the hit song *Eleanora*? There was enough evidence of foul play to convince state troopers to investigate the matter. Following a record-breaking blizzard that left much of the high country without electricity or phone service for a week, they burst into a mountain fortress, guns drawn, expecting a grim ending to the tale of the wisecracking cowboy and the frosty television goddess.

"Instead, the two were found effecting a *rapprochement* over a lazy breakfast of pancakes and homemade jam".'

'I thought you said it was coffee cake?' Murphy interrupted.

'It *was* coffee cake,' Ben answered with a frown. 'Be quiet and let her finish.'

"'In a truly intriguing denouement, both the cowboy and the lady have maintained a steadfast silence about the events that led up to their interrupted morning tête-à-tête. State trooper Raymond Daniels, however, hasn't been as reticent. 'The first thing Kolter did when we burst into the room was to push the lady behind his back to protect her in case of gunfire. The minute I saw that, I knew he wasn't a hardened criminal'."

'You didn't tell us that part.' Trawler looked at Ben with interest.

'I was trying to use her as a shield,' Ben deflected the comment with a joke. 'You know how lousy my sense of direction is.'

'You're being too modest,' Ellie said, handing Ben the magazine so he could see the already famous photograph. 'I've heard there's going to be a poster made of that photograph.'

'Good God!' muttered Ben, sinking down on a nearby chair. 'I'm sorry, Ellie!'

'It's perfectly all right. I'm planning to buy one myself.' She laughed when he looked up to meet her eyes. 'Something very strange has happened,' she admitted. 'I've been offered a job. Not just any job . . .' She faltered momentarily before the impassive smile on Ben's handsome face. 'A television station in Los Angeles wants me to host a morning talk show. It seems that four years of the best journalism school in the country isn't half as impressive a credential as having been discovered in a certain romantically attractive cowboy's bedroom.'

It was an incredible job offer, better than anything she could have hoped for, but she would have given it all up if Ben had wanted her to stay. All he had to do was ask, and she'd stay by his side for ever.

'Congratulations, Ellie.' Ben smiled as he

stepped forward and lifted her chin to lightly kiss her nose. 'When do you leave Boulder?'

'In two weeks.' She tried valiantly to hide her disappointment. 'That brings up the next order of business. I have a goodbye present for you.' She opened her bag again and took out an envelope, handing it to him. 'I hope you like it.'

He opened up the envelope and skimmed the legal document inside before he met her eyes with incredulous surprise. 'This is a release form.'

'Yes.' She couldn't help her grin. 'I know what it is, Ben. I'm the one who asked the station manager to sign it.'

'This is a release form for Ellie's tapes,' he explained to the other members of the band. 'We can use any tapes of Eleanora Martin's reviews, in part or in full, for . . .' He scanned the document again. '. . . free?'

'Not exactly,' she admitted. 'Somewhere on the video you have to display the call letters of WQBX. The station recognises free publicity when someone points it out to them.'

'All right!' Trawler laughed as he played an exuberant drum roll to greet the news. The only member of the band who didn't seem to share the excitement of the moment was Murphy, who frowned down at the weathered hand that lightly strummed the strings of his guitar.

'If you use the tapes of my reviews, you have half of the video already filmed,' Ellie continued evenly. 'How long will it take us to do the rest of it?'

'Us?'

'Why not?' she challenged him. 'Do you think you can find a better Eleanora?'

'No.' Ben's mouth quirked upward into an appreciatively warm smile. 'I surely don't, Miss Eleanora Martin.'

CHAPTER ELEVEN

ELLIE rode slowly down the slope, her white mare leaving shadowed tracks behind them on the pristine surface of the snow. Get it right, she warned herself, forcing a look of dreamy stillness across her face. The cameras were recording her trek from the ridge to the ice-coated aspens at its base, and they would have only one chance to record it over untracked ground.

Dressed in a midnight-blue medieval gown edged with ermine, she was pretending to be a princess traversing a fantasy wilderness of ice and solitude. She didn't turn around to look, but she knew that four chestnut-coloured horses had appeared along the lip of the ridge above her.

Ben had surprised her with his efficiency. In just two weeks he had put together all the costumes and hired a director and a crew to film the video. The weather had been perfect in the high country, and just two days of filming had provided almost enough footage from which to cut and interweave the dream sequence through the tapes of her reviews.

'Nicely done, Ellie,' the director complimented as she reined in the mare at the grove of aspens and slid down from her horse. A few moments later the four chestnut-coloured horses thundered up and were reined to a stop by four barbarians dressed in a picturesque assortment of ragged skins and Viking helmets.

Ben wore fur leggings that were tied in place by criss-crossed lengths of rawhide strapping. His skin vest was open half-way down his chest, exposing a large gold amulet that caught the oblique rays of the setting sun. 'You're cute for a savage,' Ellie teased him as he slid down beside her and rubbed his bare hands to ward off the numbing effects of cold. 'Come here,' she offered, circling his wrists to coax him closer. 'Put your hands underneath my arms.'

The video had been hard, cold work for all of them, but the four men in the band had had the worst of it. At least she was half-way dressed.

'You're a hot-blooded wench, aren't you?' laughed Ben as she tucked his hands firmly into her armpits and put her arms down to return the warmth to his stiff fingers. 'Why aren't you freezing like the rest of us?'

'I have more common sense than the rest of you,' Ellie answered, stepping forward just enough so that her thigh touched his. 'I wore thermal underwear. Do you want to see them?'

'When you loosen up, you don't go half-way, do you?' he laughed appreciatively, leaning down to kiss her mouth with a touch that promised more than teasing lightness.

'Okay!' the director interrupted before their affection could deepen to a more tempestuous passion. 'Save that for the next scene. Let's shoot fast before we lose the light.'

The crew moved to the untrammelled glade

they had chosen earlier and Ellie took her place in front of her white mare. Ben was right about her, Ellie thought, reaching up to stroke the horse's velvety soft nose. When she got involved with something she didn't go half-way.

In the past two weeks she had done more than simply get the tapes and agree to appear in the video of *Eleanora*. She had gone over the storyboard with Ben, suggesting better ways to interweave the scenes, and changing the direction of the dream sequence within the story. Ben had listened, quietly at first, then with more enthusiasm as he had realised that her ideas were good.

And when she fell in love she didn't go half-way, either. She loved Ben so deeply that she could feel the echo of his very heartbeats as if they beat inside her chest. She would have given up everything if he had loved her as much as she loved him. But she knew he didn't, and she wouldn't spoil what they had right now with useless demands he couldn't meet.

'We're shooting, Ellie.'

This scene had been her suggestion, and she was eager to get it right on the first filming before they lost the delicious tangerine glaze of the mountain sunset that would bathe the scene in a soft, romantic light. Ellie didn't have to pretend the dreamy sadness on her face as she pressed her cheek against the mare's soft nose. She needed only to think about the end, the moment when she would have to face the future without the unexpected love that had changed the course of her entire life. Without Ben. The words were as chilling as a mountain frost, as cold as death itself.

Ben emerged from the thicket of ice-shrouded trees. She pretended not to notice as he came closer and closer to her, stalking silently across the glistening snow. He reached out to touch her shoulder and she didn't have to pretend the shock of electrical excitement that his touch could so easily provoke.

His fingers curled around her shoulder, biting into the soft velvet fabric of her dress as if he expected her to run away in fear.

'Great!' the director called. 'Sink to your knees now. Just the way you rehearsed it at the house.'

Ben's hands pressed down against her shoulders, coaxing her to her knees in the powdery, soft snow. Ellie felt the warmth of his chest behind her as he knelt, too, and put his arm around her like a captor's bond. Then she felt his fingers tugging at her hair, releasing the hairpins one by one until her hair cascaded down across her shoulders like a shimmering stream of gold.

No words were spoken as he turned her in his arms and met her mouth with a slow deliberateness that worked its magic on her senses. His lips were warm and soft, earnestly entreating a response. She closed her eyes and gave herself up to the longing he could weave around her with the simple tenderness of a touch.

'I love you, Ellie.' His voice was a whisper, so hushed and low it seemed like a ghostly wind blown off a distant mountain, but his breath was as warm as spring against her ear. He laid her back against the snow and leaned down to take her mouth again, this time with a hunger that shook her senses and filled her with an answering excitement that could not be contained.

The snow was cold against her shoulders, but she barely noticed that. She was too caught up in a surging wave of passion to notice anything except the mouth that covered hers, inviting and demanding in equal measure as he carried her beyond the brink of pleasure to the nearest boundary of ecstasy itself.

'Terrific! That's a wrap, guys!' Ellie blinked in stunned surprise as Ben stiffened and pulled his mouth away. She had lost track of time and place in the excitement of Ben Kolter's arms. And so had he, she understood as he met her passion-clouded eyes with a wry smile of sympathy.

'We have to stop meeting like this,' he joked as he put his arm around her shoulders and pulled her up beside him, holding her with an affectionate possession that felt as natural as the air she breathed. 'Could somebody get this lady a blanket before she catches pneumonia?' Murphy tossed him a quilt, and a moment later Ben was wrapping her in a soft cocoon of warmth.

'What about you?' asked Ellie, concerned. It had been like that for the past two days. Ben had been far more careful about her comfort than about his own.

'You finally managed to warm me up,' he teased, growing more serious as he met her accusing stare. Was everything a joke to the cowboy? Ellie wondered. 'I'm okay, love,' he said reassuringly, touching his fingers softly to her cheek. 'Just as long as you are.'

The crew milled around, putting away equipment

and loading the horses into waiting vans. The sun
had slipped behind the mountains, and the
tangerine-coloured smudges of the sunset were
giving way to the violet hues of dusk. It
was almost over now, Ellie thought, moving
unconsciously closer to Ben's side as he gave
directions to the band and crew. He held his arm
around her in a casual gesture, then coaxed her
along beside him as they made their way down
the snowy slope to his waiting car.

The film was good. And it got better every time
they went over it, cutting and shaping the scenes
until they wove a romantic fantasy to fit the
building excitement of the music.

The members of the band lounged around
Ben's recording room, watching the process with
fascinated interest, but it was clear that Ellie and
the director were the only two who clearly
understood the process of editing a film.

'Let's give Ben a longer close-up here,' Ellie
suggested, studying the screen with a squinting
intensity as she tried to assess the effect of each
decision. 'Stretch his close-up by two seconds, and
take the time from the long-shot of me coming
down the slope. That might make the scene more
dramatic.'

'It might,' admitted the director as he deftly
made the proper cuts and re-ran the film. 'Your
girlfriend knows how to make you look good,
Kolter.' His eyes were still focused on the screen,
but he spoke to the man who stood silently behind
them. 'If I were you, I'd give her a job with the
band.'

'I'd make a great video director,' Ellie agreed only half-teasingly. 'Maybe I could fly out from Los Angeles at the weekends.' Ben didn't answer.

He hadn't made a comment for the last several run-throughs of the film, Ellie realised, turning now to meet his troubled eyes. Had she taken over too much? she wondered. She had only done it because she had experience with television and a natural eye for what would look good on the small, square screen.

'The lady's already got a job,' Ben answered evenly, taking one last swallow of his beer and moving away to toss the empty can into the waste paper basket. Ellie watched him curiously as the director bent above the control panel to start the video from the beginning. The newly edited version of the video filled the television screen, but Ben no longer seemed interested in the film.

He had been photographed from the back as he opened the creaking door of Murphy's living-room and crossed with weary strides to the battered television set. 'Ben Kolter's comeback performance might more aptly be described as a throwback performance,' Eleanora Martin's image flickered to life on the colour monitor. 'Most of Kolter's music fits into the My-baby-left-me-and-the-cat-is-drunk category of country primitive. The fans who have been waiting ten years for this man to return will be woefully disappointed . . .'

Her words faded out and were replaced by the opening refrain of *Eleanora*. Then her image faded, too, and was replaced by a lonely figure on horseback against a vast expanse of snowy, mountainous terrain. Four chestnut-coloured horses appeared above her on the ridge. It was this cut that they were trying, and Ellie turned around to study the screen with objective interest.

G.T.'s close-up was first, with his Viking helmet ridiculously askew. Trawler, whose scowl had more to do with the rigours of riding bareback than with any barbarian emotions, had a close-up next. Then Murphy, and finally Ben appeared. The longer close-up worked beautifully, Ellie realised, smiling with satisfaction.

Ben sat his horse with stiff-spined dignity, his dark eyes trained relentlessly on the woman who was traversing the snowy slope below him. When he spurred his horse into motion there was no question that he was going after the woman that he wanted and that nothing on this frozen earth would stop him.

Then they were in the grove, the camera trained on Ellie's sad-eyed face as a shadowy figure wove its way across the ground behind her. A hand fell against her shoulder and her face reflected the first jolt of electrical excitement.

'Nice acting,' the director muttered appreciatively. 'You could have a career on either side of the camera, Eleanora.'

It wasn't an act. The trembling desire that marked her face so strongly was so intensely real that Ellie glanced away, embarrassed that her most private feelings were so openly exposed. She turned around to see if Ben had reacted with the same shy embarrassment to the scene, but he didn't meet her eyes. 'I'm going upstairs for a cup of coffee,' he said as he walked to the door. 'Anybody want anything?'

'No,' the director answered distractedly, studying the screen.

Ellie waited only a moment, then she slipped away to follow Ben up the stairway to the kitchen. 'Can I join you for a cup?' she asked as he poured out a cup of hot, black coffee at the kitchen counter.

'Sure.' He took down a second cup and filled that, too.

'I didn't mean to take over the video,' she apologised, guessing at the reason for his disapproval. 'I just have some experience, and I was trying to help. I'm sorry if I've messed it up.'

'The film's a work of art,' he interrupted tersely. 'As for taking over . . . well.' He gave a shrug. 'We've always had one firm rule in this band: if you can do it better than the next guy, then go ahead and do it.'

So he wasn't angry at her for taking over the editing. But he was angry about something, Ellie knew, sipping her black coffee. 'What have I done to upset you?' she asked bluntly.

'It's not anything you've done. I just hate goodbyes, that's all.'

They didn't have to say goodbye. 'I'm going to Los Angeles, cowboy,' she reminded him. 'Not to the far side of the moon.'

'It might as well be the far side of the moon,' he disagreed, glancing restlessly away. 'Why don't you ask Murphy what happens when you put a few miles between two people? No,' he changed his mind, '*I'll* tell you. I'll give you an absolutely accurate prediction of our future.'

'We'll call each other every night. Maybe that

will go on for a few weeks, but sooner or later you'll get hung up at a meeting and forget to make the call. And I'll be angry because I waited all night for a call that didn't come. Or maybe you'll be out with a man,' he shrugged matter-of-factly. 'Or you'll call me and realise that I'm with a woman. Sooner or later it will come to one of those.'

Not if they loved one another, Ellie thought, sipping her coffee to soothe her pain-tightened throat. She didn't like to think of him in another woman's arms, but she knew how attractive he was to women.

'We'll start fighting,' Ben continued in an eerily quiet voice. 'We can't have a relationship over a telephone. Hell, it's hard enough for a man and woman to have a relationship when they're in the same room.'

'We could be in the same room,' Ellie suggested weakly. The only way to keep the love they had was to stay together. But there would be a price. She had worked hard for the chance that she'd been given to test herself and taste success, but if she wanted Ben she'd have to turn her back on her own ambition. She'd have to sacrifice her career the way he'd once sacrificed his for the child he loved. It was a cruel, hard choice to make, but she already knew that she would make it if he asked. 'I don't have to accept that job in Los Angeles.'

'Not accept it?' Ben echoed her plaintive words. 'For which you'd want what? Marriage?'

'That's one possibility,' she replied haltingly. Of course she wanted marriage! She had just offered to give up everything for him! But Ben's eyes darkened even more and he shoved his hands into his pockets as he turned away.

'I've been married. That's no picnic, either.'

'I'm not like Laura,' she protested. 'I'm not like any of Murphy's wives, either. I know all about the strains of the entertainment business.'

'Then you should know better than to think we've got a chance to make a marriage work,' he responded bitterly. 'There are willing women everywhere. You'd find their phone numbers in my pockets and their lipstick on my shirt collar. Sooner or later you'd start to wonder if I'd been faithful to you. And I won't have been,' he warned. 'Every time I walk out on a stage, I make love to other women. You can't compete with that, and if you tried to stop it I'd end up hating you. Oh, God,' he muttered desperately, running his hand across his forehead in a weary gesture. 'I've already destroyed my daughter, Ellie. I don't want to hurt you, too.'

'We love each other,' she suggested hopefully, feeling her heart constrict inside her at Ben's desperately unhappy words. His first marriage had ended tragically, but that was no reason to give up hope. Love was a miracle that could solve every problem, no matter how bleak and difficult life seemed. 'We can find a way to make it work.'

'You're not listening to me, Ellie.' Ben shook her reassuring hand away from his tense arm. 'I don't want to make it work.' He met her eyes for one long moment in which she could read a conflict that seemed to be tearing him apart. 'I don't love you,' he blurted out at last, glancing restlessly away to avoid the sight of the tears that sprang too quickly to her eyes. 'I didn't want to say that,' he admitted painfully. 'I was hoping I wouldn't have to.'

'But you said . . .' He didn't love her. The words had pierced her like a sword, bringing with them a sharp, agonising ache. 'Didn't you tell me that you loved me?' she demanded. 'Just this evening?'

'I didn't mean it. It was the kind of thing a man says when the affair is over so you won't think it was cheap and meaningless,' he admitted honestly. 'I care about you, Ellie. But it's not the kind of love I'd have to feel to make a marriage work.'

Ellie's throat tightened with a dry, harsh pain and her eyes were hot with tears she vowed she wouldn't shed. He didn't want to marry her, and she had made a fool of herself by suggesting that he might.

'There's no future for us, Ellie,' Ben went on in a relentless, regretful voice. 'There never was. We both knew that from the start.'

It was the truth, she knew, forcing her tears back. He had never promised anything, but he had given her affection and excitement. She was grateful for those gifts at least.

'Well . . .' She took a breath to calm her trembling nerves. 'You're right, of course. I don't know what I would have done if you had said yes to my proposal. I probably would have come to my senses and run away. I have no regrets, Ben.' She held out her hand. If they had to end it, it would be best to end it cleanly and quickly, she decided as his warm fingers curled affectionately around hers. She already knew that there would be no phone calls and no letters. There would be no strings of any kind connecting them together, no arguments or resentments to mar the memories of a love affair that had existed only briefly, then flared out like a lovely skyrocket against a darkened sky.

'You were a good lover,' she said quietly, wondering if he had taken the same exultant delight in her body that he had so generously given her. She had loved him with an unbounded heart, but he hadn't allowed himself to love anyone, in any way, since Becky died. She wondered if that made a difference to a man.

'You were the best, Ellie.' He answered the unspoken question in her eyes. Then he put his arm around her and coaxed her close, holding her with a gentleness that only served to make her sadness grow to a keen anguish as the reality of leaving him grew clear.

The next two hours passed in a haze of activity and movement that Ellie noted only with a numb distraction. The video was finished, all except for a few last polishing touches that the director was going to take care of on his own. Everyone had left the house except Ellie, Ben and Murphy. And Murphy was pulling on his coat.

'Would you drive Ellie back to Boulder?' Ben asked with a pretended casualness she knew he didn't feel. 'She's got some packing to do.'

'Sure thing.' Murphy seemed surprised. 'When are you coming into town?'

'I'll be down on Saturday,' promised Ben,

finding Ellie's coat in the hall cupboard and holding it out for her. She managed to slide her arms into the sleeves, although she barely noticed what she was doing. Her plane left for Los Angeles on Friday, and Ben knew that as well as she did.

They had already said goodbye, she understood, attempting a weak smile as Ben's hand fell softly on her shoulder in a sympathetic touch. Another goodbye would only cause more pain. Still, it hurt to know she wouldn't see him again, would never be caught up in his warm arms or look into the deep brown eyes that could stop her heartbeat with a tender glance.

Murphy glanced from one face to the other, noting Ben's hard-jawed remoteness and Ellie's evasive, tear-veiled eyes. 'Why don't I warm up the car for a couple of minutes?' he suggested shrewdly.

A moment later Ben and Ellie were alone. Ben's hand still lingered on her shoulder, and his fingers curled to hold her tight. 'Have a good life, lady.'

That was it? Ellie couldn't help a smile of bittersweet amusement as she turned to meet his eyes. Of all the parting words he could have chosen, he had chosen those?

And what was she to say? I love you with my whole heart and soul? And I always will? She had already made that clear, but it hadn't changed the cruel course of their destinies. Maybe if she had met him before there had been a Laura, there would have been some hope. But Ben had tasted the bitter fruits of marriage, and he knew better than she did how difficult life was.

'You, too, cowboy,' Ellie answered, lifting her mouth to his for one last soft caress.

Then it was over. His arm lay loosely at her back as he escorted her to the door and then across the driveway to Murphy's Ford station wagon. But they had already taken leave of one another, and not even the warmth of his touch could bring them back together. She didn't say goodbye when he leaned down to shut the door behind her.

'This new job of yours?' Murphy asked her curiously as he started the car with a grinding lurch. 'Does it have anything to do with reviewing music?'

'No,' she answered, glancing out of the window at the man who stood at the edge of the driveway with his hands shoved deeply into his trouser pockets. She was leaving him, but she knew from the empty ache she felt inside that she had left her heart behind.

'Good,' Murphy answered as they made the first turn in the winding mountain road that cut off her sight of Ben. 'Then it's safe for us to play Los Angeles some day.'

CHAPTER TWELVE

IT HAD been an uneventful show: one psychiatrist plugging his new book on executives and stress, an actor, a singer, and a nutritionist who had done a cooking demonstration. Tomorrow she would interview two actors, a ventriloquist, the national Frisbee champion and a woman who trained dogs to perform in dog food commercials.

And the day after, the same thing again, Ellie thought, smiling as the closing music played and she turned to shake hands with her guests. Mimes and authors and inventors would follow singers, playwrights and exercise experts in a long row that seemed to stretch outward to eternity. The ratings were good, and she knew she was successful. But she certainly wasn't happy.

'It's a wrap,' the director called, and Ellie stood up, walking to the studio audience to shake hands. It was a practice she had initiated a few months before and everybody seemed to like it.

'It was a wonderful show, Miss Martin,' an older woman complimented.

'Thank you. I'm glad you liked it.'

A teenager was next, and Ellie could predict the question. 'What was it like to work with Ben

Kolter's band?' The girl's eyes were wide with eager awe. 'On their video, you know?'

'It was a lot of fun. They're all very nice people.'

One after the other, she shook hands and answered questions until she reached the back of the studio and reached out automatically for a large, calloused hand.

'Don't suppose you'd have coffee with a country boy?'

She looked up, astounded, right into Murphy's laughingly amused blue eyes. 'Of course I would!' She slid her arm through his and pulled him through the doors into the hallway. 'You look great,' she complimented, gesturing him to follow her into her dressing-room. 'The band is doing very well, I hear.' She kept up a line of nervous chatter as she gathered up her bag and the notes she'd need for the next day's interviews. 'Two country music awards, and I understand that the band's latest single is expected to go platinum. It's a nice song. I've heard it on the radio.'

She had heard it everywhere. *Dusky Sunset* had transcended the boundaries of country music and had shot swiftly to the top of the popular music charts as well. It was the best song Ben had ever written, and he sang it with a clear, strong voice that made love sound like a freshly discovered emotion, not the cliché it could have been in the hands of a less gifted artist.

'Yeah, well.' Murphy shrugged. 'I guess we're doing okay. Ben's working like he doesn't know there's anything else to do, but that's how Ben has always been. What did the shrink on your programme say about the kind of man who works too hard because he doesn't see any reason to stop and smell the roses?'

'He called them obsessive-compulsive personalities. How's Ronnie?' Ellie changed the subject abruptly as she led Murphy upstairs to the employees' cafeteria. Anything was better than discussing Ben, although he was the only subject she wanted to discuss.

'She's doing real good. She's a freshman at the University of Arizona now,' answered Murphy proudly. 'We're doing a concert there next month.'

'That's wonderful! And the others?' Ellie asked as she bought two cups of coffee and nodded to a table at the far end of the room. 'Let me see if I can remember all of their names. Nathan and Steven, and Jacob and Cleantha. And . . .'

'Benjamin.'

'Yes, of course. Benjamin,' Ellie answered nervously, too aware of Murphy's curious blue eyes. 'How are they?'

'They're all fine, too,' Murphy answered as he tore open a sugar packet and poured it into his steaming coffee. 'So . . .' He gave her a smile. 'You've done real well for yourself here. I saw your picture on the back of a bus yesterday. You know you're successful when you get your picture on a bus!'

'I suppose so,' Ellie answered. Her ratings were good, and she'd just been offered a fat rise. But she wasn't happy. She had reached the top of the professional ladder and she had found success far lonelier than any of the rungs along the way. 'I have a baby brother now,' she changed the subject quickly. 'Did you hear about that?'

'I sure did.' Murphy's eyes crinkled with approving smile lines at the corners. 'They say your daddy's fit to burst with pride. An old buck like him having himself a baby!'

'He's cute,' Ellie admitted as she sipped her coffee. 'The baby, I mean, not my father. I saw him when I went home for Christmas.' He was wonderful, Ellie thought, filled with an aching longing she had tried so hard to fight. He had fitted so naturally into the crook of her arm, and he had looked at her with a wide-eyed adoration that had melted all resistance to his charms.

'You should have one of your own,' Sara-Jean had suggested. 'You'd make a good mother.' She would, Ellie knew, filling with a regretful sadness when she remembered the small hand that clutched her finger so trustingly. She would have given anything to have a child of her own lying easily against the crook of her bent arm. A child with Ben's dark eyes and attractive, quirking smile.

'Ellie?' Murphy touched her arm to recall her from her melancholy thoughts. 'I was asking if you've seen our concert yet? Tonight's our last night in L.A.'

'Oh.' Ellie's hand trembled and she tightened it around the cup. 'No, I haven't seen it.' She stopped, unwilling to tell him how much she still loved Ben Kolter after all this time. 'It's been sold out for every performance.' Then she glanced restlessly away before her eyes could reveal how much she hurt. 'How is Ben?' she asked, trying to keep her voice casual and light. 'He must be enjoying his success.'

And has he found another woman to hold in his arms? Ellie wondered, but she had far too much pride to ask that. It was none of her affair, and it would hurt too much to know.

'He's doing okay,' Murphy answered evenly. 'I'd say he's doing as well as you are. Hey, look,' Murphy shifted just enough to reach into his pocket and withdrew a small white envelope. 'I've got a couple of tickets to tonight's concert. Why don't I give them to you?'

'No, I . . . I have a date tonight,' she lied. 'A man I know—he's a doctor—he's taking me to a Fellini festival. We've planned it for a long time, and I . . .'

'Oh, no!' Murphy frowned as he looked into the envelope. 'I forgot that I already gave most of these away. I only have one left, and it's not a very good seat,' he apologised, sliding one yellow ticket out and laying it on the table. 'Row W, seat 42. You'd need binoculars to see the stage. Tell you what,' he offered. 'Why don't you and this doctor friend of yours come to the auditorium tonight, and I'll have two backstage passes waiting for you at the box office. How would that be?'

'I'm not sure . . .' Ellie faltered. 'He's not a big fan of country music, and we've been waiting a long time to see the Fellini films.' And she was still too much in love with Ben to see him face to face. That was the real reason, Ellie knew.

Love had turned her into the worst kind of lying coward.

'Well, I can understand that, I guess.' Murphy surprised her by putting up no argument. 'I'll leave the passes anyway, just in case you convince your friend. My heavens,' he added, glancing at his watch, 'I've got to get going! I promised Ben I'd be at the auditorium for a sound check. Goodbye, doll,' he said affectionately, leaning down to kiss her on the cheek. 'Maybe you can catch our show the next time we're in town.'

'Maybe I can.'

Maybe she'd be over Ben the next time the band played Los Angeles, Ellie thought as she watched Murphy leave the cafeteria with his self-assured, sauntering gait. She certainly hoped so. How much longer could she go on loving a man she couldn't have?

Forever was the word that leapt into her mind, and she struggled vainly to push the thought aside. She set her coffee cup down on the table, only then noticing the ticket that Murphy had forgotten in his haste to leave.

'When dusky sunset paints the mountains . . . With a hazy purple hue . . .' Ben's voice dropped to a hushed, low whisper and the audience dropped with him, two thousand breaths stopped in two thousand throats as he sang the last verse of the melancholy song. 'With one last breath I face the darkness . . . Dreaming of my days with you . . .

'I dream myself into the darkness . . . Where

at last I'll be with you . . .' His voice trailed off,
and for a moment there was no sound at all in
the concert hall except for a muffled sniff of
tears and a soft exhalation of a communally held
breath. Then the room erupted with applause.

'Thank you.' Ben gave a quick, self-effacing
bow. Then his fingers strummed across his guitar
strings as if they had a life of their own and
itched to get on with the music.

A group of voices lifted from the audience,
demanding that the band sing *Eleanora*, but Ben
strummed the introduction to another song
instead. 'This next song is about Murphy's dog,'
Ben spoke into the microphone. 'He had a
mangy mutt of unknown parentage.'

'Hey!' Murphy stepped forward to the other
microphone. 'What are you saying about my
dog?'

'And the dog had fleas,' Ben continued
undeterred.

'That dog ain't never had no fleas!' Murphy
shot back with pretended outrage.

'There were fleas in your house.'

'Those were *my* fleas!' Murphy answered,
scratching his full beard.

The byplay got the laugh that they expected
and they launched into a lively rendition of *My
Dog's Too Good for Fleas*, a song that highlighted
Murphy's deep, gravelly baritone and his pench-
ant for theatrics.

They had done that all evening, using Murphy's
comic antics as a foil for Ben's more romantic
voice and looks. They had moved the audience
to exuberant, foot-tapping excitement, and then

lifted them to exquisite heights with their softer, more reflective pieces. Making love to the audience, Ellie thought, remembering the way Ben had once described the pleasure of capturing their imaginations for the course of a few hours.

He made love to them in much the same way he had made love to her—alternating tenderness with a soul-stirring passion. And when the concert was over he would let them go as easily as he had let her slip away. She had no doubt that he had cared about her, but it hadn't been love, at least not the kind of love it took to make a marriage work. Tears gathered in her green eyes, and she was grateful for the anonymity the darkness gave her. She could watch the man she loved, then slip quietly away before he had a chance to see her. There would be no halting, hesitant words and no embarrassed silences to dim the memory she had of the gentle, sweet-voiced cowboy.

The song was over and Ben waited for the applause to die away before he stepped back to the microphone. But Murphy beat him to it. 'We've got a surprise for all of you people tonight. The boys and me have collected all the ticket stubs and we're going to have a raffle.'

'A raffle?' Ben demanded with amused bewilderment. 'What are you going to raffle off, Murphy? Your dog?'

'Nothing that good. We're going to give away . . .' Trawler beat a drum roll. '. . . a date with Ben Kolter,' Murphy announced. 'Or with me if the lucky lady prefers . . .' The rest of his words were drowned out by the exuberance of the audience's applause. Ben didn't seem entirely comfortable with the proceedings, but he said nothing when G.T. brought in a ten-gallon hat and held it out in front of Murphy.

'And the winner is . . .' Murphy made a drawn-out production of fishing in the hat for a ticket stub and squinting at the numbers. 'The lucky winner of a date with Benjamin Kolter, the King of Country Music, is the person sitting in row W, seat 42. Can we have a light on the lucky winner, please?'

It was her seat, Ellie realised, blinking as the spotlight suddenly illuminated her.

'Who is it?' Murphy asked, squinting out into the audience. 'We need binoculars to see way back there.'

'Oh, God!' Ellie slid down farther in her seat as people craned around to see her. Then she was recognised.

'It's Eleanora Martin!' somebody yelled up to the stage. The cry spread as other people recognised her tear-streaked face and soon the audience was chanting, 'Eleanora! Eleanora!'

'Hey! It's Eleanora Martin!' Murphy said delightedly as Ben walked to the edge of the stage and stared out past the sea of faces. 'Well, this is some coincidence. Come on up to the stage, doll. We'll sing our favourite song for you.'

This was no coincidence! This was a publicity stunt, Ellie understood. The crowd was even louder now. 'Eleanora! Eleanora!' they were calling, and Ellie felt herself fill with a mindless panic. The tears were flowing down her cheeks, and her mascara was completely smudged. She couldn't walk up on that stage and pretend she didn't love Ben Kolter. Nor could she pretend she wasn't furious at the callous way that he could use her for publicity after everything else that had happened between them.

'Excuse me,' she mumbled. She was on her feet with only one thought in mind—to get away as quickly as she could. But Murphy had given her a seat in the middle of the row and she was stumbling blindly over feet and knees. Finally she reached the aisle.

'Ellie!' A shout tore through the cacophony of voices. It was Ben who called after her, but Ellie didn't stop. She ran up the aisle and pushed through the doors into the lobby, so shaken she could barely think. A moment later Ben burst through as well. 'Ellie?' His voice was hoarse and trembling. 'Are you all right?'

'Don't touch me!' she warned, stepping back when he reached out to take her in his arms. 'How dare you do that to me without any warning!' Tears welled up and coursed across her cheeks. 'If you wanted cheap publicity . . .'

'I didn't,' Ben protested, as distraught as she was now. 'I didn't even know that you were here.'

'I would have put you on my show. Why didn't you just ask?'

'I couldn't! I couldn't see you and pretend that I don't love . . .' Ben stopped suddenly, embarrassed by his unexpected revelation.

'What?' Ellie met his eyes with blank bewilderment.

'I didn't want to see you . . .' He glanced restlessly away to hide the tears that gathered in his own eyes now. 'Because . . .' His fingers tightened into angry fists and he turned away completely. 'Damn! I'm going to kill Murphy for this stunt. I told him to leave the situation alone.'

'You love me?'

'No!'

He was lying. He loved her as much as she loved him, but she had been in too much pain to see that truth before. Now she saw it all, but she still couldn't understand the reason for his defiant denial of his feelings. 'Do you love me, Ben?' Ellie repeated firmly as she moved in front of him and seized his arm. His tight mouth and evasive eyes were all the answer that she needed. 'Why can't you say the words to me?' she pleaded, reaching up to touch her fingertips to his tear-streaked face. 'I love *you*.'

'We can't make it work, Ellie,' he answered painfully, catching her hand to pull it down from his wet cheek. 'I gave up my music for ten years, and I remember how hard that was to do. I can't ask you to give up what you love most.'

He meant her career, she realised, understanding his sacrifice at last. He had let her go because he loved her too much to ask her to make a choice, and she had gone, following the glitter of a career that now seemed as lonely as an ancient, far-off star.

'You're more than Ernest Martin's unwanted daughter,' Ben whispered painfully. 'I wanted you to find that out.'

'And now I've found that out,' she agreed, clinging to his shoulders. 'I'm the woman that Ben Kolter loves.' She met his brown eyes with so much earnestness he stopped and studied her eagerly hopeful face with the hesitant rebirth of hope. 'Will you marry me, Ben?' she demanded.

'You'd have to give up your career to follow me around the country.'

'All right.'

'I'd want kids.'

'You bet,' she agreed so quickly he stared at her in stunned surprise.

'You hate my music,' he reminded her.

'You're getting better.' She tightened her hold around his shoulders and stepped forward until her thighs pressed close to his. 'So . . .' She met his eyes with all the love that had been rekindled by his touch. 'Are you going to marry me, Ben Kolter? Or are you going to tell me you don't love me enough to take the chance?'

'I love you,' he admitted in a voice that vibrated with emotion, 'more than I've ever loved any other woman.'

'Is that a yes?'

'You bet.' His mouth twitched outward into a widening grin. 'Tonight? Before you come to your senses?'

'I've already come to my senses, cowboy,' Ellie answered lifting her face to invite the ecstasy of his mouth against her willing lips. Their mouths touched softly for a moment, then Ben's arms tightened to coax her closer. He deepened the caress until they fell downward through desire and beyond it to a realm of feeling where their hearts and souls were bound in an eternal pact of love.

'You don't know how good it feels to have you in my arms again,' he admitted in a whisper, pressing his face against her smooth, blonde hair with such devotion that her heart stood still inside her tightened chest. What she wanted was so clear she knew she'd never regret her choice.

'Yes, I do.' Her arms were around his shoulders holding him so close she didn't know where the boundaries of her own body ended and the boundaries of his began. She was home where she belonged, home in the circle of Ben Kolter's arms, and she had no desire to ever leave again. 'Don't let me go, cowboy,' she insisted. 'Don't ever let me go.'

How long they stood there locked in their embrace, Ellie didn't know. But finally she rose again through all the complex layers of their love. She slipped her mouth away from his and pressed her face against his throat where a throbbing artery beat out a rhythmic echo of his heart.

She could hear the drumbeat from the concert hall, and Murphy's gravelly, low voice like a windborne cry from a far shore. 'I had me a horse and a six-gun . . . I had me a pretty good life . . . I had me the stars and my freedom . . . But then I took me a wife.'

'Did Jesse James take out the garbage?'

'What?' Ben stirred enough to meet her eyes.

'Isn't that the name of this song?' she asked. 'Did Jesse James take out the garbage? Did the

Kid eat humble pie? Did Sundance wear a suit on Sunday? Then why on earth should I?'

Ben's mouth stretched out into a grin of understanding. 'You've heard my new album?'

'Once or twice.'

'Once or twice?'

'Okay,' she admitted honestly, 'I own the album. But don't tell anyone.' She lowered her voice to a teasing whisper. 'Marrying you is one thing. Singing your songs in the shower is quite another.'

She felt the laughter in his throat and pressed her mouth against it in a richly devoted kiss. Here was her happiness, she knew. And it had always been here waiting for the moment she was capable of seeing it for what it really was.

Ben loved her as much as he loved his music. Maybe more, she realised as she looked up to meet his radiantly happy eyes. But he didn't have to choose between them. 'You have a concert to finish,' she reminded him, reaching up to touch the softness of his face. 'Go make love to your audience, Ben. You can make love to me later.'

'All right,' he agreed reluctantly, putting his arm around her to coax her to a door that led into the backstage area. 'Don't run away,' he ordered when they reached the wings. 'Stay right here where I can see you until the concert's over.'

'I will,' she promised happily as he leaned down to kiss her mouth. 'And if I do run away, you come after me and drag me back.'

'Don't worry about that,' he promised firmly. 'You're not getting away from me again.'

She stood in the shadows of the wings as Ben walked out on stage and lifted his guitar to slip the strap around his neck. The audience was hushed with expectation as he walked up to the microphone. 'The next song is about a lady who's got a country cowboy wrapped around her little finger.' He strummed his fingers across the strings, playing out the introduction to the song. 'I'd like to dedicate it to a woman who has just signed on with the Travelling Asylum Band as video director.' He cast a quick glance in Murphy's direction, grinning as he noted his friend's anxious curiosity. 'And the lead singer's wife.'

'It's about time!' Murphy gave a laugh. He strummed the strings of his guitar and Trawler beat a quick tattoo against his drums.

'Whoa!' G.T. stamped his foot.

'I watch the news for Eleanora . . .' Ben's voice lifted in exuberant delight as the audience erupted in applause. Then all four voices joined in the first chorus of the rowdy cowboy song. 'She won't tell me any lies . . . I watch the news for Eleanora . . .' Ben looked towards the wings, meeting Ellie's glance with a smile that fell against her like a touch. 'And I undress her with my eyes . . .'

Harlequin Presents

Coming Next Month

1023 TOO SHORT A BLESSING Penny Jordan
After the tragic death of her fiancé, a young Englishwoman becomes
convinced that she'll never fall in love again—until she meets a very
determined man who has every intention of changing her mind...and
reaching her heart.

1024 MASQUERADE MARRIAGE Flora Kidd
On a Caribbean cruise, Carlotta discovers that the deckhand paying so much
attention to her is really a bodyguard hired by her wealthy father because
of kidnapping threats. The complication of their falling in love is not part of
the plan.

1025 CIRCLE OF FATE Charlotte Lamb
Things get complicated when Melanie, already doubtful about her
engagement to a prominent businessman, meets another man who infuriates
her, but also attracts her. Breaking off her engagement, however, doesn't
immediately bring about the desired results!

1026 A RACY AFFAIR Roberta Leigh
Emma Fielding, governess to a racing car driver's motherless child, is
persuaded to marry him so there'll be a guardian in case of his death. When
they fall in love with each other, they're too afraid at first to admit it.

1027 OUT OF THE SHADOWS Sandra Marton
When Lauren meets the man she knows is right for her, past bitterness
between their families threatens their love. Can they selfishly ignore the
hurtful consequences of their actions to achieve a happy future together?

1028 BRITTANY'S CASTLE Leigh Michaels
Successful banker Brittany Masters reluctantly agrees to a mock reconciliation
with her unfaithful husband until he obtains a government appointment. In
return he'll give her a divorce. The situation is awkward, but happily nothing
turns out as they expect.

1029 NO STRINGS ATTACHED Annabel Murray
When lively, actively social, travel agent Vita, believing in love and commitment,
meets attractive but footloose Dominic, looking for a temporary affair, conflict
is inevitable. So, too, is love—but in between is a time of turmoil.

1030 TOUCH AND GO Elizabeth Oldfield
That it turns out to be a hoax, doesn't make her stepfather's kidnapping any
less harrowing for Karis, visiting him in Bangkok. Especially when the only one
she can turn to is the man she'd loved and broken off with six months before.

Available in November wherever paperback books are sold, or through
Harlequin Reader Service:

In the U.S.
901 Fuhrmann Blvd.
P.O. Box 1397
Buffalo, N.Y. 14240-1397

In Canada
P.O. Box 603
Fort Erie, Ontario
L2A 5X3

Can you keep a secret?

You can keep this one plus 4 free novels

ATTRACTIVE, SPACE SAVING BOOK RACK

Display your most prized novels on this handsome and sturdy book rack. The hand-rubbed walnut finish will blend into your library decor with quiet elegance, providing a practical organizer for your favorite hard-or soft-covered books.

Only $9.95

Approximately 16" x 8" when assembled

Assembles in seconds!

To order, rush your name, address and zip code, along with a check or money order for $10.70* ($9.95 plus 75¢ postage and handling) payable to *Harlequin Reader Service*:

Harlequin Reader Service
Book Rack Offer
901 Fuhrmann Blvd.
P.O. Box 1396
Buffalo, NY 14269-1396

Offer not available in Canada.

BKR-1A

*New York and Iowa residents add appropriate sales tax.

Harlequin Intrigue
Adopts a New Cover Story!

We are proud to present to you
the new Harlequin Intrigue cover design.

Look for these exciting new stories, which mix a contemporary, sophisticated romance with the surprising twists and turns of a puzzler . . . romance with "something more."

Plus . . . we are also offering you the chance to enter the Intrigue Mystery Weekend Sweepstakes in the October Intrigue titles. Win one of four mysterious and romantic weekends.

Buy the October Harlequin Intrigues!